· A ·
GOOD·BOOK
· IS · THE ·
PRECIOUS
LIFE-BLOOD
· OF · A ·
MASTER
SPIRIT
Milton

PRINTED IN GREAT BRITAIN

The KINGS TREASURIES
OF LITERATURE

GENERAL EDITOR
Sir A·T· QUILLER COUCH

LONDON : J·M·DENT & SONS LTD.

'SHAG'

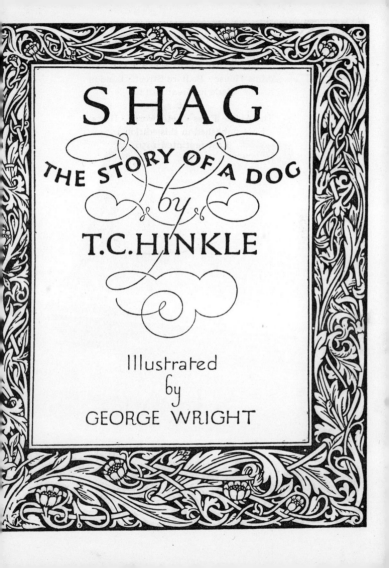

SHAG

THE STORY OF A DOG

by

T.C. HINKLE

Illustrated
by
GEORGE WRIGHT

D 239/62 m

CONTENTS

CONTENTS

ILLUSTRATIONS

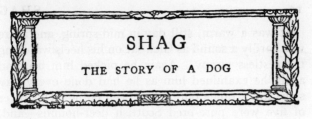

SHAG

THE STORY OF A DOG

CHAPTER I

THE THROWBACK

THE faintest little whining cry attracted Tom Glen's attention as he tightened the saddle on his horse early that morning. Glen paused and listened as the horse switched his tail in protest to the girth. Again came the faint whining cry. Glen let the horse stand and walked quickly inside and to the south end of the long ranch stable. He smiled as he stooped and picked up a little blind, helpless puppy, eight days old, that had got out from the others.

'Here, you little rascal!' exclaimed Glen. 'What's the matter with you, getting away like this?' and he put the little pup back in among a litter of four others that had all been sleeping peacefully after the mother had gone out a little before. 'You keep quiet with the others,' said Glen, and he sat on his heels watching this singular, imperfectly-coloured puppy. He was still restless, and would not sleep like the other four.

It was a warm, still day in mid-spring, and there was hardly a sound as Glen sat on his heels watching the restless puppy. Again he picked him up, and again he examined him as he had done every day since this strange puppy had been born. This litter of five were pure-bred Scottish deer-hounds—and, oddly enough, all five were males. The restless little pup had been named Shag by one of the men because already he had much longer hair than his more favoured brothers. But this was the least of his trouble, for he was so ill-coloured for a pure-bred Scottish deer-hound that Glen at once decided against him. He held the pup tenderly in his big hands and finally said with deep regret: 'He 'll never do. He 's a throwback. Impossible for my purpose of breeding pure-bred deer-hounds'. Then as he still held him he thought to himself: 'I 'll keep him a few months, until he 's big and strong, and one of the men will take him off my hands'.

Glen put the yellow and white spotted pup, with the snow-white head, back with the others, but he still sprawled and whined in his restlessness. The morning being warm, the little pup could not have been cold, and he had nursed all he wanted from his mother a little time before. No, it was not cold and it was not hunger—the only two things that stir the ordinary week-old puppy to move and whine. It was something in this little ill-coloured, shaggy - haired pup that foreshadowed unusual vitality in both mind and body.

Little Shag, as he moved restlessly among the others, stood out in marked contrast to the perfect colouring of his brothers. They were all what is known as 'self-coloured', that is, each of one colour only. One was a dark blue-grey, one was cream, two were sandy-brown. But poor little Shag! He had large spots of white and yellow over him, so that it was difficult to tell which colour predominated, and his head, as mentioned, was snow-white. His tail was about half-white, half-yellow, and Nature, as if trying to be wholly unkind to him in his outer appearance, gave him at birth an unusually long, harsh coat. His little stubby legs already gave evidence that, when grown, he would have unusually long hair clear down to his toes.

Of course, Glen mused to himself, this colour is impossible, and it is also plain that he is going to be a big, awkward dog, with an altogether too long, harsh coat of shaggy hair. 'Too bad,' said Glen, turning away. 'I had hoped they would all do, but I 'll find some man that I can give him to later on.'

Three more weeks passed. The pups were a month old. Shag was now a happy, even if a homely, little creature. The fun spirit was always in him. He proceeded joyously to awaken his brothers many times each day. He was now much bigger than any of them, and certainly always more lively. He would pounce into the middle of the sleeping ones and nip them and pull at them until all were awake. At this he would begin one of those romps which did not stop until Shag became too enthusiastic with his puppy teeth and one of his brothers would loudly cry out his protest. Always at such times—Tom Glen and the men had all seen—old Flora, the mother, would get up and walk quietly over to Shag, lift him up by the nape of the neck, robust though he was at this time, and set him down beside her as she again lay down. Shag understood, and here he would remain, slowly blinking his puppy eyes, turning his head from side to side, while intently watching the others.

Shag was now old enough to explore his little world, and life was always a joyful thing to him. He nursed his mother and lay long hours beside her, curled up in the warm rays of the sun, his sides rising and falling as in the peaceful sleep of a child. And, oddly enough, the little shaggy pup was always in a place by himself when beside her. The others at this time all lay together as she curled around them; but little Shag, after he had nursed, and it was time for his nap, would walk sleepily around old Flora's front legs, and then she would lie with her head very close to his, his little white head resting on her lower forelegs. His ill colour, his hair far too long, and his stubby little big-jointed legs made no difference at all to his mother, and sometimes, while he slept, she seemed, if possible, a little more solicitous about him than the others, for as often as he breathed a long sighing breath, after the manner of sleeping puppies, his mother would nose him affectionately and sometimes caress him gently with her tongue.

So the days passed. Sometimes two or three times a day Tom Glen came to look at his pups, and as often as he came he squatted down and played with Shag, for it was always Shag that came up ahead of all the others to play with him. As the weeks went by, and as Shag grew in body and mind, he became more and more attached to Tom Glen. Finally, after he was four months old, he would go up to the ranch-house each night and sit at the door and wait, sometimes an hour, for Tom to come out. The moment Tom appeared Shag was all smiles. He would leap up on Tom, and Tom would slap his sides good-naturedly, and Shag would be in an ecstasy of joy. Yet in all this Tom Glen never once understood, perhaps no man would have understood, the possibilities born in this dog. And the only reason Glen had not parted with Shag before was because he had promised him to a man who wanted him, but who had been delayed on a

trip to the east—a circumstance which could not
be foreseen and which, to make the story brief,
caused Tom Glen, in the end, to keep Shag until
he was two years old.

So there grew in Shag a greater and always
greater love for Tom Glen, and Shag knew nothing
whatever, of course, about the plan to give him away.

As he grew bigger and stronger he did not know
that he was more and more growing away from the
type of the pure-bred, and that more and more he
showed that he was a throwback, as men called it,
to some foreign strain. Shag only knew that from
morning until night he was always happy just
because he could be with Tom Glen. Shag remembered him first of all men because, when his doggie
consciousness first came, it was the hands of Tom
Glen that were upon him and around him.

Tom Glen, in these swiftly-passing days, never
once considered the real merits in the case because
he did not know them. Glen wanted only the finest
strain of Scottish deer-hounds, and his feeling towards
Shag was not dislike at all. Tom really liked him,
yet felt at the time that it was a mistake to hold
him so long for his friend. Incidents of Shag's
puppy devotion might have been seen time after
time, for they were unusual. Shag might be lying
down with his shaggy, stout forefeet holding a bone,
and he might be gnawing ever so joyously, but if

SHAG WAS DEVELOPING INTO A TREMENDOUSLY BIG DOG

he heard the voice of Tom Glen he would stop, prick up his ears and point his nose to locate the sound, and *leave his bone* to run up and try to tell Tom how glad he was that he could be with him.

So Shag grew bigger and stronger, his hair grew more shaggy, his young legs showed knotted joints, and as he grew his whole build made him awkward and clumsy. The other dogs, on the other hand, were developing into perfect specimens of their strain as to colour and size and form.

Yet Tom still kept him, for time after time his old friend Pete Bently, who had gone east, wrote about the dog, and Pete was delighted to know that Shag was developing into a tremendously big dog, since that was what interested him most, he said. But still Pete did not come, and still the weeks and months drifted by, until Shag was two years old. Each week and month of this time had drawn Shag more and more to the man he loved.

There was one place in particular to which Shag loved to go with Tom Glen. This was a beautiful little valley with its stream and a near-by slope on which was a clump of pines surrounding what was known as Glen Springs. And as often as Tom halted to drink from the spring and rest, and allow his horse to drink and feed near the stream below, Shag would go in the shallow water of the brook and drink his fill. Then he would come up to Tom

Glen, smile happily at him, and go back along the
stream to nose the green fringes of grass and willows
and so spend a little time; but always, after a little
of this, Shag would return to Tom Glen, and there
he would sit down and look at him and await Tom's
least word or action.

It was on this little slope, with its two tinkling
springs and silent grove of pines, that Tom Glen
came most often to rest and wait during the two
summers that had now passed in the life of Shag.
That first summer carried with it sweet memories
to Shag, but he was so young then that he forgot
some of them. Not this second summer, however.
Every part of it—the little springs, the green grasses
along the stream, the cool comfort of the water to
his hot and weary body, and finally the tall pines,
sometimes sighing in the wind above the man he
loved—this was all very sweet to Shag, and especially
because so many times it was here that he had the
man all to himself. The other dogs, of perfect type,
seldom stayed longer than to drink their fill at this
place, when they would set out for home, letting
Tom Glen come when he would. But it mattered
not to Shag how long Tom Glen might sit at the
Glen Springs and rest and even doze a little, as he
did now and then—Shag was always there and very
close to him. And then the moment Glen stood up
and prepared to mount his horse Shag was ready

also. It made no difference how tired or how hungry he was.

Now there came one day, to Tom Glen's great surprise and sorrow, a message telling him of the accidental death of his friend, Pete Bently. Pete Bently, for whom he had so many months kept Shag and kept him for this reason only. Tom was very much depressed at the death of his friend, and it was several days before he again thought of his problem concerning Shag. Glen had never once during this time entertained the thought of keeping him for the reason mentioned, and now he was sorry that Shag had not been put in another home at a younger age.

Tom pondered the matter for a time, then picked out a man he was certain would give him a good home and gave Shag away. But Tom Glen discovered that this was a difficult thing to do. He gave him away three times in as many weeks! Time after time he sent Shag to distant ranches, but each time Shag managed somehow to escape, and, once free, he set out in a straight course for Tom Glen. Again he was given away, and this time he was securely chained, but he set up such a persistent uproar day and night that at last the man let him loose. Shag raced for home and came in almost exhausted. He was still a young dog at this time, and the full meaning of it all did not come to him. Not understanding, he came leaping up on Tom Glen, as if trying to say: 'Oh, see! I got away from that terrible place! I thought of you and only you day and night! What terrible men those were to try and hold me away off there!'

After this, other and urgent business occupied Tom's attention for a time and two weeks passed. Then Shag was given to a ranchman who took him up into the distant Sweet Briar region and managed to keep him for three months. But the reason he stayed those miserable months, it was agreed on all hands later, was because Tom Glen had stood over him at the distant ranch that day, and while the ranchman held Shag, Tom scolded him, even shook a whip at him, and told him he must stay.

Shag was older now, and this, for the first time, went to his heart. Although given his liberty the next day, Shag did not try to go home. He lay in the yard, his eyes closed, listless to all the world. If one of the men came up and spoke to him he would open his eyes and pat his tail gently on the ground once or twice, but that was all.

At the end of two weeks Tom met one of the men and told him he was glad Shag had found a place where he would stay. 'Take good care of him,' said Glen, 'he's a very friendly dog.'

It was under these adverse circumstances that Shag was first taken out with a pack of dogs to

hunt grey wolves. It was nearly noon when two
big grey wolves started out of a *coulée* and every
dog in the pack, including Shag, gave chase.

Twice before, when Shag had been out with Tom
Glen and some of the younger dogs, a grey wolf had
been started up and they had run a little, but not
far, because Tom Glen had ridden behind them and
scolded and called until they came back. They
were too young, he said, to endanger themselves at
the fangs of one of these experienced, deadly fighters.
That was four months before. Shag was now, of
course, just that much older, and the men on the
hunt on this day believed thoroughly that all the
dogs, including Shag, should rush blindly into the
fight. They did not as yet know as much about
timber wolves as did old Bob McKee, the trapper.

It was now for the first time that this strange,
untrained throwback dog acted a part that was as
singular as his size and colour. Shag was far
heavier than the ordinary deer-hound, weighing
fully one hundred and thirty pounds, yet, in spite
of his big joints and awkward, ambling gait when
walking, he possessed, oddly enough, a speed
greater than the other hounds, but he was slower
at starting.

Shag was a little behind the main pack of some
ten dogs when the wolves started out a considerable
distance away, but he raced out and in time passed

the foremost hound. Then the odd thing—Shag drove for the nearest enemy, as he did so throwing up his head and using his powerful chest as a battering-ram. He actually bowled the big wolf over, but leaped clear as the beast whirled and slashed at him; then Shag stood away while the other dogs blindly closed in. The wolf cut two of them to pieces and was off before the men, who had seen it all, could ride up. Once again, however, Shag, running hard behind the wolf, knocked the beast nearly from its feet, but again Shag leaped clear and stood by. Both wolves escaped in some dense timber and scrub, and the men heaped anathemas upon Shag for not rushing in like the other dogs. A dozen men poured out their wrath in hot words as Shag turned panting from his hard running and trotted away. The old trapper, Bob McKee, who rode with them this day, was Shag's only defender.

'He's too smart,' said Bob. 'He's young and not experienced, and he knows it. Some day he may fool you.' But McKee's remarks were met with protests of disgust and anger from the men as they looked upon their badly-slashed dogs.

Thus matters stood for a time. Tom Glen was much disappointed when Shag came back. If Shag could not be used at wolf fighting no one would want him at all. During the next week Tom spoke to several of the ranchmen about taking Shag, and when they said he had proved himself no good, Tom tried to take Shag's part by saying the dog was still young and that later on he might prove a great wolf fighter. But for a week Glen had no success at all, and he was provoked to think Shag was still with him, still following him, no matter how far he rode, and sometimes Glen rode hard all day.

Tom Glen was but twenty-eight, a bachelor, with blue eyes, a shock of blond hair, and although a young man of wealth, he was one of the hardest-working, hardest-riding men on the range. Yet no matter how far he rode it was never too far for this singular dog, Shag, to follow.

Late one evening Tom Glen, followed by his pure-bred hounds and Shag, pulled his horse to a stop at the beautiful spot known as Glen Springs. Dismounting, he drank from one of the springs under the tall pines. Glen was very tired, and as he was no great distance from home, he sat down to rest a little. All the hounds but Shag, seeing that Glen was going to stop here, at once started home. Glen watched them with a pleased expression on his honest face. There was a new female, Yellow Bird, he had bought, with her perfect colour and fine lines. There was Blue Boy, no less perfect in colour and form, and likewise the others, all

perfect in colour and build, and Tom Glen's eyes
brightened at the thought of his possession of these
dogs. A slight sound caused him to turn, and his
eyes fell on Shag standing a little away, wagging
his tail, smiling, looking with the depths of devotion
at young Tom Glen, and a frown crossed Glen's
face. He was provoked again that Shag was making
so much trouble. If he would only prove a wolf
fighter a home might be found for him. Tom Glen,
still frowning, turned his head away from Shag,
paying no attention to him, because immediately
Tom's whole mind was taken up with the business
of wondering whom to give the dog to next. Shag
ceased to smile, dropped his head, walked slowly
some ten feet away and lay down, his head on the
ground, his half-closed eyes on Tom Glen. Shag
could not leave him, and at the moment, if Tom
Glen could have known what was in those fine, deep
brown eyes, looking out from under white, shaggy
brows, he would have been amazed, and Shag would
have been to him far above all other dogs. As it
was, however, Tom did not know, but he did
remember this incident later—how cold he had been
to Shag on this evening, and Shag had stayed with
him when all the other dogs had gone home.

So Tom Glen, sincerely and honestly enough for
the time, revolved Shag in his mind, for the sole
purpose of getting him away from the pure-bred

dogs of perfect colour and size and form. As the silent moments passed Shag got up once and moved nearer to Tom, and there he again lay down. He dropped heavily to his side and with loving, patient eyes looked at Tom and waited. Shag had had nothing to eat since morning. He was very hungry, but that did not matter—now.

The silent moments passed. As Glen sat pondering the matter his eyes wandered now and then to Shag himself. He seemed more ill-coloured, more big-jointed and awkward than ever. It was at this moment that Glen thought of a man who, he believed, would take Shag. And then, for the first time, the thought came to Glen that he should keep Shag and let the other dogs go. But he put this thought out of his mind by thinking to himself that he would get a good home for Shag where the man would be kind to him. At the moment this seemed fair and reasonable to Glen. As he sat thinking it over, a blood-red sun hung poised for a time in the west, then sank behind a dark, sober cloud. Stillness lay around the little springs save for a low western wind that blew moaning and sighing through the pines.

CHAPTER II

SHAG AND TOM GLEN

It was just at this time, before Shag could be given to the other man, that Tom Glen brought in two imported, pure-bred Scottish deer-hounds, five years old. These two, both males, were, to the dog fancier, beautiful specimens—beautiful in form, size, and colour. But it happened that both of these dogs had unusually morose, even savage, dispositions. It was never Shag's way to be other than friendly to a dog if the dog would allow it. When, therefore, these two new hounds were loosed on the place Shag came up to them smiling, but they set upon him like two tigers, slashing him severely. Amazed and stung by the pain, and perhaps insulted at this sort of treatment in his own yard, Shag drove in on them, whirling, slashing, leaping, carrying the fight to both of them, when Tom Glen came running out and put an end to the fight. When Shag sat down and looked up with his fine eyes—eyes that had something pleading in them, Tom Glen said to him: 'Shag, it seems you were only born to make trouble. I'm sorry you're not a fine specimen, but you are impossible, and I must get you away from here, and I do hope you will *stay* away! It's hard to be patient with you. You should *stay* when I give you away. Bud Gordon is coming for you, and this time you must *stay away!*'

Shag only dropped prone to the ground and closed his eyes. It was that same evening that the ranchman, Bud Gordon, came for Shag. After some conversation, Bud tied a rope to Shag's collar, mounted his horse and started. Shag protested and pulled back on the long rope with which Bud held him. Tom Glen said, not unkindly: 'Go on, Shag! Be a good dog now! Go on! Bud will take care of you—go on, Shag'. Shag's head dropped and he cried, cried and started away, walking slowly behind Bud Gordon. Bud let the horse walk slowly and Shag followed, crying as he went.

A week passed, then Shag came back. He rushed in one morning early, his coat wet with dew, his eyes wide, and shining with hope. Again he was in his own blessed home with Tom Glen, and always to Shag home was anywhere this man might be. There was no road too long, no way too rough, no night too dark for Shag to find him if only permitted. When Shag came in neither Tom Glen nor any of the men were in sight. Shag started to run for the house, when he was confronted by the two surly hounds. They both drove at him, and at that

Shag was at them, slashing furiously, driving them back in a whirlwind attack, when Tom Glen came running out.

Glen, highly provoked at Shag, believed he had caused all the trouble. He scolded him severely for coming back and making so much trouble, though this morning he did nothing more than scold him, at the same time resolving to get him away again as soon as possible.

At the scolding from Tom Glen Shag walked slowly away, and lying down near what had been his kennel, he uttered a low, barely audible groan. Tom heard, however, and supposed the dog was whimpering because of pain from his wounds, and for the time he forgot the incident. Then a new thought came to Glen.

As he stood looking far to the west he could see the snow-capped peak of Thunder Mountain. In the Willow valley below, the day before, Glen had seen three grey wolves. The dogs had not been with him. Why not take Shag out with the other hounds and try him after the wolves? If he made good at fighting wolves, someone would surely keep him.

Hours later Tom Glen rode alone toward the valley of the Willow, Shag and the two older hounds of the morning fight running alongside.

It was nearly noon when, as Tom rounded the

head of a grassy swale, an old grey wolf, caught napping in the warming sun, leaped out only a short distance away. Glen yelled to urge on the dogs, at the same time putting spur to his horse. The two older hounds rushed, and so did Shag. It was fair running, and in a short time the two older hounds were trying to close in. Shag, thus far, had run neck and neck with them, but he now shot out with an amazing burst of speed, threw up his head and, using his chest as a ram, nearly bowled the wolf over, but then leaped clear and stood by as the other two hounds slashed the wolf and were themselves badly slashed in return.

It was a running fight for a mile. Three times the wolf, a seasoned fighter, ran clear and three times Shag rushed ahead, threw up his head and rammed the wolf, bringing him to a stand, but each time Shag leaped clear and did not drive in. He received one slash on the shoulder, but he shot clear so quickly the fangs of the wolf got him only slightly. The wolf escaped in an impenetrable jumble of rocks and down timber.

Tom Glen looked at his two older hounds with their many wounds and then at Shag with but one slight one. And Tom did not understand. He believed Shag was simply afraid to fight wolves. Time, of course, would tell. He must give him to other men. They could try him.

Several weeks passed, weeks which Shag spent away from Tom Glen because he was chained up at the ranches of three other men, but each time that he got loose he ran all the way home. And each time that Shag came home there was always a dangerous fight with the two imported dogs, for they still set upon him when he came and they always attacked him together. Of course this made no end of trouble for Tom Glen, and Tom's only idea was to get Shag away and somehow keep him away—that he honestly believed would end all the trouble both for himself and Shag.

Shag was next given to Joe Gun, a ranchman forty miles away. Joe led Shag to the ranch, put him in a small shed and locked the door. All night Shag gnawed at the boards with his powerful fangs, and in the first of the dawn Joe came out only to see the big dog with the white head crowd out through the opening, where he had gnawed a board to splinters, and streak toward the north—and the home of Tom Glen.

It was a long, weary journey for Shag, but he made it, made it only to find himself, three days later, at the ranch of Abe Blackmar, where Tom Glen took him. Shag was here chained securely. Then Tom mounted and started away, but Shag struggled and cried so loudly that Glen came back and, as he said afterwards, tried to reason with Shag.

Again Glen started away, and again Shag cried out to go with him. Then Tom, almost exasperated at what, to him, seemed inexcusable rebellion on the part of Shag, came back and scolded him soundly, telling him he '*must* keep still'.

At this Shag dropped to the ground, and he did not move or utter a sound as Tom rode away. He only lay and quivered and shook as if in a chill, though it was not the cold, for the day was warm and still. The sun was shining, the air was balmy and sweet with the odour of wild flowers in the valley; but Shag's world was cold and bitter, and there was only night and storm there. He knew fully now that the man he worshipped and loved did not want him, but Shag could not give him up—he could suffer on and on. No matter what Tom Glen did to him he never, never, never could cease to love him, and so all this was hard, so terribly hard. Shag did not even turn his eyes toward Glen as he rode away. There was no use. He only lay very still, paying no attention to the physical world around him.

Abe Blackmar wanted Shag, for he believed he might yet prove a great wolf dog—possibly the dog that had so long been needed to fight with the huge yellow lobo wolf that for two years had been a terror to the cattle and range horses.

Abe chained Shag to a wire staked to the ground

This wire was fifty feet long, and it permitted the dog to run from one end of it to the other by means of an iron ring.

Now Blackmar had a pack of seven dogs of large size, all of mixed breed except one, a Russian wolf-hound. All of these dogs, except the wolf-hound which bothered no one, set upon Shag and fought him almost every day. Chained as he was, Shag might have been killed more than once if it had not been for his reach, from shoulder to head, his mighty jaws and cutting fangs, and above all his brain that here, as in fights with other dogs, developed a plan of battle which the average dog never knows. It was not that Shag liked to fight. He detested it with his whole being. But he had to fight, and if he had to he could, with an imagination and a skill seldom witnessed in the wilds of the west.

Abe Blackmar as yet did not know this. He was solicitous for Shag, and if he heard sounds of fighting he would run up and with shouting and kicking drive the dogs off. Once he caught two of the trouble makers and gave them a sound beating. Abe was afraid they might kill Shag when no one was near.

At last, however, so tempestuous and dangerous did Shag become in these fights that, handicapped though he was by the chain, the dogs only passed

B

him with bristling manes and snarls, as Shag,
towering up near the biggest of them with his
powerful body, curled back his lips, making no
sound, but letting all see his deadly, gleaming
fangs. The dogs all knew him now. And Abe
noted that he heard no more sounds of fighting—
only low, guttural, deadly snarls.

Blackmar lavished all the petting and kindness
that he knew on Shag, taking him out for a long
run each evening at the end of his chain; and then
at the end of three weeks Abe saddled his best horse
one morning, and after feeding Shag and caressing
him, and holding one end of the chain in his hand,
said: 'Come, Shag! I'm going to take you with
the dogs this morning and hunt the old yellow lobo'.

Abe mounted, called all his dogs and started,
Shag following without trouble at the end of the
chain.

In the late evening of the day before Abe had
seen the tracks of the big lobo in the sand near the
Canyon River. When about two miles out on this
day Blackmar dismounted, petted Shag and un-
snapped the chain from his collar, letting him go
free. Again Abe mounted and started on the hunt.
Shag, after a little hesitation, wagged his tail and
followed.

The other dogs ranged out well ahead, but Abe
would call them back every now and then. The

yellow lobo had already killed two of Abe's dogs
and Ben Bowers had lost one in this way. Shag
did not travel much ahead of the horse. He would
trot along, his long tail and mottled form seeming
in awkward contrast to the agile ease with which
the other dogs moved. Now and then Shag would
look up at the face of Abe Blackmar, and if only
Abe could have seen it, there was unhappiness
written in the deep brown eyes looking out from
the shaggy brows of that broad, white head.

Suddenly Abe reined in his horse, at the same
instant jerking his rifle from its holster on the
saddle. With a low whistle he called all his dogs
close. He saw on the margin of a sandy draw the
certain trail of the lobo. The wolf was headed east
toward the more open country. Abe thought rapidly
and planned his course. He had seen the day before
the carcass of a young bull on which wolves had
been feeding. He would approach this against the
wind. As he started he turned and looked quickly
to see if Shag was coming. He was, but stopped
and seemed timid when Blackmar looked at him.
He came on, however, when Abe spoke to him.

For a mile Blackmar rode along the bottom of a
long, sandy *coulée*, keeping his horse at a jog-trot
and not permitting any of the dogs to surge ahead.
Arrived at the base of the low ridge, just beyond
which was the carcass of the young bull, Abe turned

sharply from the draw and rode into a narrow cut in the ridge, with Shag and every other dog for the moment at his heels.

A stiff wind was blowing in Abe's face as he approached from behind the cover of the hill. Hoping, yet doubting, that there might be one of the wolves feeding at the carcass, Abe put spurs to his horse and rode out of the cut at a run. To his great astonishment not only one wolf but two were there, one a black wolf, the other the giant yellow lobo himself! It was the first and the last time that a rider ever came to such close quarters with the lobo. Blackmar jerked his rifle to his shoulder and fired at the big wolf, but with the horse running missed. He did not get another chance to fire at the lobo without great danger of hitting some of the dogs, but as the black wolf veered off Abe fired rapidly and by a lucky shot killed him. With scarcely a pause he spurred hard after dogs and lobo, spurred and lashed the horse into his best, for every dog in that pack was in great danger once the lobo came to a stand.

To Abe's disgust the big wolf was quickly out of sight in a rough region of rocks and high ridges. Then, as the rider topped a high ridge, he saw the dogs and the dangerous lobo in a thrilling, running fight. At this moment Blackmar cried out in anger and disgust at the action of Shag. He shot ahead

of the foremost dogs, and using his chest as a ram,
struck at the big wolf so hard against the hips that
he turned him clear around, but Shag leaped clear
and did not rush in blindly as the other dogs did.
If at this dramatic moment Blackmar had understood Shag he would have had a profound admiration
for him; but neither Abe nor any of the other men
of the range understood. They all believed, as Abe
did, that the only way for a dog to fight a wolf was
to rush in and fight and kill or be killed. Wolf
hunting with dogs had gone on but a few years
here. Much was still to be learned.

Only the oncoming, yelling Abe kept the lobo
from coming to a complete stand and so making a
massacre of the dogs. He ran on, and for the first
time in his life kept an eye on a single dog—a dog
that had not tried to rush in on the wolf, but had
done a strange thing—rammed him clear around
and leaped away so quickly he could not reach him.
But Blackmar did not know. It was a case where
a dog knew more than a man. Shag ran on when
the lobo ran, and in less than a quarter of a mile he
again performed that strange trick and leaped clear
as the lobo's fangs this time grazed him, cutting
through the skin. Although he was now fully
grown and a big and powerful dog, Shag was still
young, and his instinct said to him on this eventful
day: 'Don't rush in on this beast like the other

dogs! He will kill you if you do! Go slow!
Watch him! Guard with your fangs!'

Whooping and yelling, Abe rode hard after his
dogs. There was a brief space when he could not
see them, and then after a time he came upon them
where the dogs had all stopped. They were lying
down on a little stretch of level valley. Every dog,
excepting Shag, was badly slashed, although none
dangerously. Shag lay a little apart from the
others on some stony ground, his head up, his
great red tongue hanging out while he panted for
breath.

Abe Blackmar was angry because the lobo got
away—got away when he had been so close to him.
Got away with likely never such a chance again.
And, after his impetuous manner, Abe was angry
at Shag. He turned on him and scolded him
harshly, telling him that of all the dogs he was a
coward—that not once had he dared to rush in.
Then Abe, honestly supposing he was right, bent
over first one of his dogs and then another, petting
and praising them and at the same time saying that
he would not keep such a cowardly dog as Shag.
Abe, moreover, said to himself that he would drive
him back to Tom Glen if he tried to follow.

But when Abe finally mounted and started he
found he had no need to be troubled about the big
dog. When he turned to look he saw Shag in the

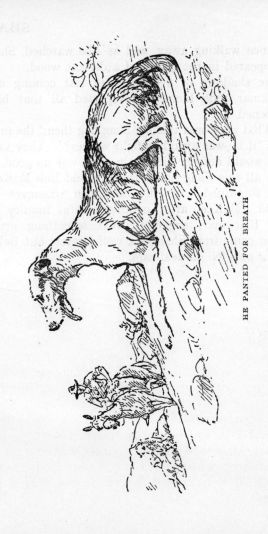

HE PANTED FOR BREATH

distance walking away, and as Abe watched, Shag disappeared in the gloom of a distant wood.

The shadows of evening were fast coming on. Blackmar rode home and reported all that had happened.

'What good was this big Shag dog then,' the men said, 'if he was afraid to fight wolves?' They said they would not try him again. He was no good.

In all this Shag had a friend in old Bob McKee, who sojourned with the ranchmen whenever he would. McKee, after making careful inquiry of Abe Blackmar, suggested that something great might come from Shag as a wolf hunter; but Bob's words now fell on deaf ears.

CHAPTER III

A STRANGE WOLF HUNTER

AN unusual thing happened in the life of Shag when he left Abe Blackmar that day. He did not at once go back to Tom Glen. It may be that for the first time he believed there was no use for him to go back because he could not remain. Something of the kind must have been in his brain, for over a week passed in which no man in the Tamarack region saw him. Then he turned up early one morning at the ranch of Link Pedlar over in the valley of the Rim Rock.

Link knew Shag and instantly recognized him. He also knew that it was believed generally among the men that the big dog was afraid to fight wolves.

For some reason unknown, when Shag appeared among strange dogs there was always a terrible fight, and so it was that Link Pedlar on this day ran out near one of the stables to witness one of the fiercest he had ever beheld among dogs. Link had two big Russian wolf-hounds, not so big as Shag, but big nevertheless, and they were older

* B

dogs than he. Their one single purpose in rushing
in for a strange dog was to kill him as quickly as
possible, and woe to the lone dog out on the plains
who could not escape! But here they had a surprise.
Shag drove in and attacked them furiously. It was
a whirling, rushing attack toward Link Pedlar's
ranch-house and not from it. When Link had
beaten his dogs into their senses and stopped the
fight he looked upon the two white wolf-hounds,
slashed and bleeding, and at Shag who did not run
away, but stood bleeding also.

As Shag stood there he was thin, his ribs were
showing, and Link understood. He came up and
put his hand on the big white head. 'Well, Shag!'
he exclaimed. 'They're all talking about you and
saying you're a coward at tackling wolves. Maybe
they don't know. Come, I'll feed you!'

Shag was desperately hungry. He gulped down
the pieces of meat and corn bread that Link gave
him, and when he had eaten he looked up and
wagged his tail slowly in a quiet, appreciative
manner.

Shag could not have come in at a better time for
Link Pedlar's purpose. Link already had saddled
his horse preparatory to going on a wolf hunt.
And now he petted Shag and talked to him for a
time, and then said: 'You're just in time, Shag!
You will follow now! I know you will—come!'

And as Link swung in the saddle and started he found that Shag did follow. The other dogs let him alone and he trotted behind.

When this day passed it passed with tragedy, for when Link Pedlar rode into his yard that night it was without one of his best dogs—a wolf-hound killed by the lobo. It seemed that now the big yellow wolf might be started up with dogs, but only at a distance. On this day he had been started far out in the hills by the dogs, and he had left only a trail of wounded dogs and one killed to tell the story.

Link Pedlar, however, had seen the chase clearly at two different points when dogs and lobo ran across open ground, and twice Link saw Shag rush ahead of the other dogs, throw up his head and ram with his chest, then leap clear and not go madly in as all the other hounds did.

Link Pedlar, like the other men, did not stop to think that Shag was still young. And if he had, it would have done no good. Other dogs his age had rushed in on the wolves, and some of them got killed, too, but honest Link Pedlar, like the other men, knew nothing more for a dog to do. A great fighter, one that had the keen brain to know the need of plan and cunning, he had never seen. To Link and the other men all dogs as wolf fighters were much the same, except that some dogs rushed in harder than others. Link rode into the yard at the ranch that night and threw the saddle from his sweating mount as two men came up. One of them was a regular rider of Link's, and the other, by chance, old Bob McKee, who had come in for supper.

'Ran that big wolf again to-day,' said Link. 'He killed one of my best dogs. That Shag dog's not worth a whoop. I took him along, and when I started the wolf he kept right up with the other dogs and most of the time he was ahead of them, but the minute the lobo whirled to fight Glen's dog would leap away. Then, when the big wolf would start running again, that dog would run right up behind, throw up his head, ram the lobo with his chest and almost bowl him over; but he was away like a cat when the wolf came at him. When I got up to the finish and found one of my dogs dead and saw Glen's dog standing off just panting, with his eyes shut, I got so mad I threw rocks at him, and I was mad enough to kill him, too, but of course he's still Tom Glen's dog. I tell you he's no good—he's afraid to fight wolves!'

At this juncture old Bob McKee, who had been listening, spoke up: 'Well, boys, maybe you're right and maybe not—can't always tell. But my guess is that that big Shag dog's got plenty of pluck. He's got too much sense to fly into the lobo the way all the dogs you ever knew fight wolves'.

This suggestion of Bob's was met with scorn by Link Pedlar. He said heatedly: 'Bob, you know about the foolishness of that dog as well as we do, and you're the only man that stands up for him. What makes you think that there's anything in him? Just think of the dogs that have been killed'.

'All the same, Link,' said old Bob kindly, 'I'll hold steady a bit—I've had heaps of dogs—and dogs is terrible different—as different as men. Mind you, I don't say I know about Shag, but just the same I'm not ready to condemn him—yet.'

'But *my dog got killed* by that wolf to-day,' Link began.

'Yes, Link,' old Bob interrupted, 'and maybe Shag knew that there would be more dead dogs, including himself, if he went at that dangerous beast like your poor dog and so many others that have closed in on that lobo. My guess is that Shag's waiting—something in him tells him to wait—and whatever it is that tells him, it's that which makes him understand how he must fight that wolf, if the time ever comes when he has a chance.'

'Then you mean he's not *afraid* to fight the lobo,' Link exclaimed.

'I'm not saying I know—yet,' said old Bob, 'but Shag certainly knows he mustn't fight like the common run of dogs. And while I reckon I can't blame you and the rest of the men of the range because you say none of you will ever feed Shag or allow him around again, I do say that my guess is you may be mistaken about him. I don't say I know—not yet!'

So the matter ended, for the time, that silent evening on the Link Pedlar Ranch. Link with the others profoundly believed that Bob McKee was all wrong. They believed that Shag was a coward.

As the evening sun sank low in the west that night Bob McKee sat alone in the yard of Link Pedlar. 'Shag's never had a chance yet,' he mused, 'never had a chance; but none of these fellers can see it—knocked the yellow lobo over and leaped clear before the snake could strike! Done it to-day, and done it now a number of times in their hunts for that beast. That Shag's not like the other dogs. He *knows*! *They* don't! He knows, and he's just beginning. What will he decide to do now with every man driving him away? Thunder! If I could get hold of him before I start up the river for the winter trapping I'd take him. But next week I'll have to start, and no telling where Shag'll be—then.'

Then old Bob McKee uttered strangely prophetic

words. He said: 'If Shag lives and Tom Glen lives, there 'll come a day when Tom Glen will see that he has made a great mistake, and when that time comes Tom Glen will feel so bad he can't eat. I know him. Tom 's got a heart as big as an ox. The other men don't know him—yet '.

CHAPTER IV

THE LONELY HEART

FAR to the west, where the Little Aspen River
wound and murmured its way through a long, quiet
woodland, lay the horse ranch of Ben Bowers. Here
there were great sweeps of broad uplands, and here
and there great hills that looked down on deep,
wild, pine-clad canyons with their crystal streams
flowing along the bottom.

It was here one morning, in the heart of this
region, that Shag next turned up—at the ranch of
Ben Bowers. Why he did not go to the home of
Tom Glen after the happening at Link Pedlar's was
still a mystery. Many believed afterwards that he
was like a lonely boy, knowing he was not wanted
at home, yet at the same time making a brave effort
to endure his life in a strange land. At any rate,
by another turn of chance, just as Ben Bowers and
his men were preparing that morning to go out to
hunt wolves with the dogs Shag came in.

Ben Bowers' eyes opened wide with pleasant
anticipation. 'Look here who's come!' he called
loudly, 'that big Shag dog of Tom Glen's. They all

say he won't fight wolves. Let's give him a try with *our* dogs!'

When Shag came up in the yard several of the dogs bristled up to him, but when Shag stood tense, his fangs bared, they walked away snarling, manes bristling, and let him alone.

In a little time all was ready. The men swung into their saddles and there was some brief pitching of half-tamed horses. They galloped out on the valley, a dozen dogs running in front of them. Suddenly Ben Bowers pulled up his horse. 'Wait!' he shouted, 'that Shag dog's not coming!' Ben rode back and was at considerable pains to persuade Shag to come along. Shag seemed listless, with no interest in things like the other dogs. At last, however, after Bowers urged and insisted, Shag followed him.

The men, led by Ben Bowers, rode until well along in the afternoon, but no wolves had been brought down. Two had been seen at long distance and the dogs had given chase, but nothing had come of this. Then came good luck. Two wolves were caught unawares near a bend of a stream, and there the men quickly brought them down with rifles. There seemed hope now that other scourges of the cattle and horses might be destroyed.

Several miles were covered, however, and nothing happened. Ben Bowers had just said he believed

there would not be much chance that day, as it was
getting late. He was about to say that they had
better turn toward home, when a thing happened
that was like an electric shock to them. They had
just passed from an open valley into some rolling
ground covered with mesquite and low, scattering
thickets. All day the men had constantly watched
the dogs, shouting at them to come back when they
ranged too far ahead, but during the last half-hour
no one paid any attention to them. Five of them,
always more adventurous than the others, were seen
all at once, well to the north, running along a ridge,
Shag with them. A wild yell came from Ben
Bowers. 'Look! Look!' he shouted; 'they 're
after the yellow wolf!'

Shag raced away with the foremost dogs after
the lobo, and although now in poorer flesh than
the other hounds because of days of little food, he
nevertheless passed the first hounds within a quarter
of a mile, and as the lobo raced along some open
ground Ben Bowers and the men saw Shag drive in,
his head thrown up, and all but knock the running
lobo from his feet. The huge beast whirled, and
Shag, weakened from lack of food, was not quite
quick enough—he got an ugly slash in the shoulder.
The other hounds closed in. Before the men could
come up one of the hounds was killed, and the
deadly beast shot clear, to escape wholly in a wild

SHAG DID NOT MOVE FROM THE LOW HILL

tangle of rocks and down timber on the slope of the Rim Rock Mountains.

The men had seen it all. They came up furious because Shag had not gone recklessly in like the other dogs. Ben Bowers said afterwards that there was something away back in his own brain that day which told him Shag was the wise one and not he. At the moment, however, only anger and disgust toward Shag prevailed. The men set about burying the dead dog, Ben Bowers bemoaning its fate. The other hounds that had been in the fight lay on the ground near by with many wounds, but none worse than Shag's gaping shoulder. Shag lay apart from the others, his head up, the hot slaver dripping from his jaws.

The men were terribly angry with him. They said he was so big he should have gone in.

These men, like the others, said they would have nothing more to do with him, and they rode away. While Shag lay on the knoll the thumping hoofs of the horses sounded fainter and fainter. Shag did not move from the low hill. He lay there until the night came, and he began to feel very sick. He lay, head and all, prone on the ground, his shoulder stinging, a sick feeling all through him and a dull, incessant throbbing in his head. He did not know why the men hated him. He only knew that he wanted to go home to Tom Glen.

CHAPTER V

THE SEARCH

HUNGRY, lonely, his spirit pleading for what he so much desired, Shag turned, as it proved for the last time, toward the home of Tom Glen. The dawn was breaking when he started.

Now it happened that as Shag came up in the yard of Tom Glen that morning Tom was out on the West ·Valley with his field-glasses looking for a stray bunch of cattle, and so, unfortunately, Glen did not see Shag when he came in. Young Len Pitts, the fifteen-year-old boy who had always lived with Tom Glen, was just coming on foot out of what was known as the South Woods toward the house some distance away.

The moment young Len Pitts saw Shag he started hurrying toward him, for while the boy loved the stern yet lovable Tom Glen, he also loved Shag with all his soul, and only out of deference to Tom Glen had Len kept silent, saying nothing, but always feeling that Shag deserved more than all the other dogs together.

It happened also on this morning, while the early sun shone on a strangely-hushed world, that both the ill-tempered deer-hounds saw Shag as he came into the yard.

These two older deer-hounds, having from the first shown only hatred toward Shag, wanted more than any others to destroy him. Whenever Shag had come back home or on other occasions it was these two dogs that always started the trouble, though as yet no man knew just how it happened. When the uproar began on former occasions either Tom Glen or some of the men had come up in time to drive Shag and the other dogs apart; and always Tom Glen and his men knew these fights were dangerous—each time it would have been a fight to the death, and each time it occurred Tom Glen had been extremely provoked because Shag came back and so caused it all, as Tom honestly believed.

It happened on this morning that Tom Glen, sitting his horse, with field-glasses to his eyes, turned the glasses down the valley just in time to recognize Shag in the yard in fearful combat with the two deer-hounds. A sudden anger took possession of him as he spurred his horse toward the fighting dogs. Again, he thought, here was the dog he had tried so hard to give away—here he was again trying to kill all the dogs in the place!

Glen put his horse at a run down the valley, shouting out his imprecations at Shag as he came. And Shag! How he was fighting both dogs! They

TOM GLEN SEIZED SHAG BY THE COLLAR

were slashing him, but he was driving in so furiously with his righteous rage and ripping fangs that both his enemies together were getting the worst of it.

As Glen rode nearer, Shag, himself badly slashed, got a throat-hold on one of his enemies which would have probably meant death if Tom Glen had not leaped from his horse and rushed up. The other hound slunk away, knowing well enough he was guilty in setting upon Shag.

Tom Glen seized Shag by the collar and began lashing him hard with his whip. For a moment, however, Shag, wild with rage at this, the fourth attack of these enemies, did not notice. Then, not because the pain of the cutting whip stopped him, but because he was all at once aware of the voice of the man he loved, and that man now striking him, Shag leaped back and looked swiftly into the face of Tom Glen as the whip descended again. And then Shag, blood streaming from his great shoulders, uttered a wild, heart-broken cry and started away—started away, not howling and whining like a dog in pain, but moaning low in great agonizing sobs as he disappeared below in the silent, waiting woods. And Tom Glen, his face flushed, breathing heavily, holding the whip in his hand, stood looking; and somehow, for the first time in all this, a strange feeling for Shag came over him.

At this moment Glen was startled by the sounds of running footsteps behind him. He turned, astonished, to see young Len Pitts, pale, almost breathless, tears in his eyes. Len dashed his hand quickly across his eyes and began jerking out his words. 'Tom! I yelled at you—from the woods back there—when I started—but I couldn't make you hear. These two hounds started it—I saw it all! They attacked Shag first. When Shag came into the yard they flew at him—Shag tried to get away from them—he made for the door of the house. He bumped against the door and the two dogs drove at him. Shag was only trying to get back to you—Tom—he wasn't to blame for anything.' Len halted a little for breath, for he had run hard, then he panted out: 'I 've wondered about what the men say about Shag when they take him out after wolves—and especially the big lobo—but I don't believe Shag's a coward—and I never will! He 's still young, and he 's just too smart to run in on that lobo and get killed like the other dogs—the men just don't know—Tom! I think it 's awful the way you send Shag away—when he cares so much just for you—it 's always *you* he wants—only *you*—if he 'd only make up to me that way—I wouldn't give him away for all the dogs on the Tamarack—but he 's never wanted anybody but *you*—why don't you take him—Tom—and let him grow older and give him a chance? Why, Tom! if Shag understood it was for *you*, he 'd fight till he *died* for *you*. It 's awful the way you and the men treat him!'

The boy's voice quavered. He stopped speaking, and these two—big, strong Tom Glen the man and the courageous boy of the Tamarack—looked into each other's eyes. In that moment a feeling of perfect understanding and with it one of profound sorrow swept over honest Tom Glen. His face changed. The commercial phase of the dog business, colours, types, faded away as if these had never been. Remembrance of all his cold and miserable attitude toward Shag in giving him away came over Glen like a wave. Shag going away— going away alone now—cut and bleeding because of these two contemptible hounds—Glen felt them so now—Shag moaning in his helplessness in the face of a man who had crushed the heart of him— and Tom, that man!

Glen finally spoke: 'Len, I 've been wrong to Shag all through this! What 's the breed and colour and size of a dog, anyway? Maybe he 's gone back to the ranch of Ben Bowers. I 'll ride out and see if I can find him'.

Without another word Tom Glen mounted his horse and rode away, his horse's hoofs beating a steady tattoo in the direction Shag had taken.

But look as he would in the woods, along valley and hill-side, he saw no sign of Shag. And still he rode on and on and hunted and hunted, but again, look as he would, he found no sign of Shag. Would he now go far away, never to come back?

The sun was far down in the west when Tom Glen pulled up his horse and stopped. The late evening wind was blowing in his face and there was a croaking of some frogs in a near-by swale, but he was not conscious of the wind nor the croaking of the frogs. He had just remembered that the trapper, Bob McKee, had often told the story of a dog he himself once owned when a young man, and how that one day, due to a misunderstanding, he had severely punished the dog, who walked slowly away, head hanging, crying low as he went, and how the dog had never come back, although Bob said he had searched for many days.

But Tom said to himself that surely this must not be so of Shag. It was too late now, but on the morrow he would ride to the distant ranch of Abe Blackmar. Shag had started in that direction, and perhaps he had gone back there.

But the next day it was the same, Tom Glen found no sign of Shag, nor yet the two days following. On the third night, long after all the men had gone to bed at the Glen Ranch and were sound asleep, young Tom Glen sat alone in the great living-room

of the ranch home that he had furnished according
to his bachelor liking. There were great polished
cattle horns on the walls, many guns for many
purposes, wild animals' heads with solemn glass
eyes looking down from the walls, wild animal rugs
on the floor, and wicker rocking-chairs. In the
largest of these chairs sat Tom Glen now, while he
looked with serious face upon the dimly lighted
floor. Wealthy young Tom Glen had always had
all he wanted until this moment—and now he sat
miserable, unhappy—all because of a *dog*.

As to Shag's conduct toward the lobo, Glen's
heart was now all with Shag. 'Of course,' he
thought, 'he was too smart to go in and get killed.
Bob McKee was right. Shag knew and the men
didn't. And the reason Shag only ran after the
wolves half-heartedly was because I've taken all
the heart out of him! He wanted *me* all the time,
and never even once did I play fair with him! I
was always giving him away. He believes he can't
come back now, but I'll hunt till I find him. To-
morrow, I'll likely get track of him.'

Glen sat back in the wicker rocker and closed his
eyes, but he did not sleep. The silence in the house
was broken only by the rhythmical tick of the clock
on the mantelpiece. And outside the wind, blowing
down from the north, moaned and sighed around
the ranch-house. Autumn was at hand; the wind

was foretelling the suffering and death that was ere long to come to all living things without food and shelter. Tom Glen still sat in his chair, his head now bowed in his hands. The true Scotch heart in him was at last fully aroused to the meaning of this. He remembered how the thought of keeping Shag had flashed through his brain that evening by the springs, and he remembered how he had put the thought from him. All the emotion that ever came to a true Scotsman's heart because of his dog now took full possession of Tom Glen. He had been so engrossed with the new experiment of raising a fine strain of pure-bred hounds that he had been as blind as the blindest bat to the finest and most devoted of dogs. He knew it now, and in this still hour something came over Tom Glen, something that was to change him utterly for many and many a week to come. He wanted just one thing in the world. He wanted Shag. To the other range men this would have seemed strange that a man could feel all this *just for a dog*. In truth, this was what they were to feel after this night. And it was to make no difference to Tom Glen what the men said to him, how much they should try to argue with him and tell him he was too much concerned about all this. There was henceforth to be no peace for him until he should find Shag. As to the other dogs, Glen had nothing against them, but he no

longer had any interest in them, and it is worthy
of note that all interest in raising pure-bred dogs
left Tom Glen on this night. His mind was made
up. Shag had from the first been so glad when he
was with Glen, and to think he had given him away
time after time merely to keep dogs that were of a
pretty pattern. And these very dogs had set upon
Shag—Len Pitts had seen them—and Shag had had
to defend himself. What would a man have done
under the same circumstances! As to Shag's
fighting grey wolves, Glen now had absolute faith
in him. 'If I can find him, Shag and I together,
we 'll show them,' Glen said.

Tom Glen got up, put more wood on the fire and
stood close to the window trying to see out. When
the dawn came Glen saddled his horse. He wanted
no breakfast, and after drinking a cup of black
coffee he galloped away, to ride and ride and ride
until he should find the one dog in the world
he desired.

...

CHAPTER VI

HOMELESS

WHEN Shag left the Tom Glen Ranch that morning
he did not stop until he had covered many miles. It
was evening when he lay down in a clump of pines.
He rested here until morning. After refreshing
himself with a drink from a water-hole, he drifted
steadily westward and still westward on the upper
reaches of the Little Aspen River.

A week passed here in which he obtained only
the scantiest of food. Always he felt tired and
hungry. One morning after a futile search for
something to eat he came to a quiet dell where the
Little Aspen whispers and purls its way through a
tall and silent pine-wood. After feverishly lapping
the water here, Shag dropped down on his side under
the shade of the trees. He breathed a long sigh,
closed his eyes, and kindly Nature, for the time,
carried him away from a troubled world.

It was here that Shag made his temporary home
while the autumn days went swiftly by.

It was one evening in November that grizzled

old Bob McKee paddled his canoe into a low-lying shore of the Aspen River and made preparations for his camp for the night. McKee built his small fire, and had progressed to the point where he had finished his evening meal and was about to roll up in his blankets for the night, when he heard a noise out in the darkness that instantly attracted him. Again he heard the sound, and was certain it was the whine of a dog.

Bob turned away from his camp-fire, and looking out into the darkness, called kindly for the animal to come up. The low sounds came again, and they came closer. Then the dog came timidly into the circle of firelight.

'Oh! It's you—Shag! As I live!' said old Bob, instantly recognizing the big yellow and white spotted dog with his great white head. Shag came up and McKee petted him kindly. The dog was very poor and evidently in bad condition. Bob fed him, and after some persuasion induced Shag to lie down near him beside the river, although Shag showed plainly that he wanted to go.

It had happened that Bob McKee had left the Tamarack region just seven days before Tom Glen and Shag had met that eventful morning when Shag had come back for the last time. So McKee, already far in the wilds, did not know what had happened. He supposed that Glen, as well as

FEVERISHLY LAPPING THE WATER

the men, simply looked upon Shag as 'a big
no-account throwback', an expression usually
applied to him.

Bob said afterward that if he had known the
truth of the situation at this time he would have
certainly and gladly taken Shag all the way back
to Tom Glen. But Bob did not know. He supposed that things were as they had been—that
Tom Glen would on no account keep Shag.

While Shag lay close by, quivering a little as if he
were cold, Bob said: 'It's too bad, Shag, none of
the men will give you a home; but the great pity
is that Tom Glen, in spite of all I said to him about
you, will not have you. It's a great pity, a great
pity, indeed, seeing you've given your whole heart
to him. If you'd only stay with me—but I know
you won't! You're miserable and lonely, Shag,
you'll not stay with me or any other man, but
one—I know you. It's a pity!'

An idea came to Bob. He got up and fixed a
small chain around Shag's neck and tied him to a
little stump close by. 'Only this once, Shag,' said
Bob affectionately. 'I'll never chain you again,
but I'd just like to have you start with me up the
river if you will in the morning.'

Bob rolled up in his blankets and went to sleep.
When morning came Shag was curled up on a
corner of Bob's blanket. Bob again fed Shag, got

the boat ready and invited the dog to get in. Shag stepped in and lay down on a small canvas pack in the prow of the boat. At first, as the little craft moved silently up the stream, Shag looked with mild curiosity out on the narrow river, and now and then at the near-by banks. After a time he put his head down on the pack, and Bob McKee, facing him, noted that Shag had his eyes set straight forward, looking into vacancy, and Bob understood. He knew that Shag was far away in memory at the home of his puppyhood.

The hours went by. There was no sound save the soft dip of the paddle in the stream as Bob McKee, with the tireless effort characteristic of him, sent his canoe over the water, now in the bright sunlight and now in the cool shadows of tall pine forests. Often Bob would look at Shag, but Shag was always the same—lying perfectly still on the pack, his deep brown eyes open, but looking, as it seemed, far away. As Bob looked at him he thought to himself: 'He 'll never stay with me. He has only come this far with me because I kept him last night when he was so hungry and he wants to show me he 's a gentleman. He won't stay unless I chain him, and that wouldn't be right'.

Late that evening Bob paddled in to the shore and again cooked his evening meal, feeding Shag

again, speaking kindly to him. Then Bob again
went to his bed in the wild. When he awakened
the next morning he looked about in a little surprise,
though he had felt sure it was coming—Shag was
gone.

CHAPTER VII

ENEMIES IN THE WILD

ALTHOUGH for several years grey wolves had been destructive to both cattle and range horses in this region of the Tamarack, there were two that were especially bad. They were a dark-grey and a yellow wolf, the latter known as the Yellow Lobo, much larger than others of his kind. Five other wolves composed this dangerous pack, which in pure viciousness was probably never surpassed in the old West. Persistent hunting with wolf-hounds had brought down four of the marauders, but the dark-grey wolf and the huge yellow lobo still carried on their warfare, and more than one good dog lost his life when either of these wolves was set upon. Because three of the best dogs had died from poison, that method of killing had to be abandoned, and the most cleverly set traps had proved useless against both these cunning beasts. During the last two years these two wolves seemed to have taken a grisly delight in hamstringing horses, frequently killing the animals, while many times leaving the carcasses untouched. And woe to the range horse

that, in the winter, penetrated far into the wild,
for unless he happened to be extremely agile and
extremely swift he was certain to make food for
these two large, merciless savages.   Their pure lust
for blood was shown a year before, when on a quiet
summer night they dared to come into the corral of
Jud Weston, where there were twenty yearlings,
and although Weston was awakened with the
commotion and came out as quickly as he could,
he found six of his yearlings dead or dying and his
faithful collie dog dead with them.   But the two
wolves escaped, giving Jud only a glimpse of their
sinister forms.   Time after time these two had been
hunted with dogs and guns, but always they had
evaded their pursuers, and frequently with disas-
trous effects on one or more of the hounds, as had
been the case when Shag had been taken out to
hunt them.

There was never a time when a great wolf-
destroying dog was so much needed, and the men
had hoped that a big one would develop.   Such a
dog, with the aid of lesser hounds, would surely
bring down these two outlaws, the range men said.

Shag had offered the men their first hope, but
when, as it seemed to them, he proved the worst of
cowards, their hope of him turned to anger, and
their feeling against him just at this time was even
near to violence.   They could not tolerate the sight

of him, much less feed him. And with this feeling already so intense against him, it would only require another spark to kindle their wrath to the point of hunting him like a wolf.

This, of course, Shag did not know. He knew they had no use for him, but he did not know why, and he therefore took to the wild forests and plains alone. Shag was now a very big dog, and he was one of those dogs which, like some men, do not develop in mind very quickly, but which finally learn much more than those seeming at first to learn so easily. This trait of character showed especially now that Shag began to learn how to fight in the wild, for all were his enemies here. He learned slowly and at first painfully. He once snapped at a weasel and was badly bitten, but he killed the weasel and ate it. One evening while hunting along a stream he came face to face with a fisher-cat. Shag saw the gleaming fangs, and this time he did not rush in, but feinted for an opening; when he struck he struck like a snake, and although the fisher-cat gashed Shag's lip, Shag shook the thing to a lifeless mass, and again he fed.

Winter came, and one bitter cold night he was picking the bones of a horse's carcass, a horse the lobo wolf had killed, when half a dozen large coyotes suddenly loomed up on the moonlit snow. They circled snarling and showing gleaming fangs. They

knew Shag for a dog, and did not fear him as if he
had been a grey wolf. When they appeared Shag
was holding a thigh bone. In silence, his every
muscle tense, his lips curled back, his eyes burning,
he waited. Closer the coyotes circled, snarling,
edging in. One of these larger coyotes was alone
capable of killing a smaller dog. Shag was big, but
they were emboldened because there were six of
them. They were circling close to him, when one of
them drove in at his rear and slashed him. Like a
cat Shag shot out. It was an overwhelming, whirlwind, rushing fight. And it was swiftly over. All
the coyotes were gone, save one that lay dead on
the snow. Shag stood panting, sharp, stinging
pains cutting him in many parts of his body. One
gaping wound in his shoulder stung badly. Shag
tried to lick it and relieve the pain, but could not
reach it. Regardless of pain, he fell to the carcass
and all night stayed by the feed, sometimes crunching up bits of bones that could be heard distinctly
along a near-by creek that was bordered with strag-
gling trees. Often, as the wild things passed along
the frozen stream, they heard the crunching of
bones and stopped to look across the snow at the
big form looming over the carcass in the moonlight. Once a lone grey wolf passed by and stopped.
Long he looked and sniffed, and looked again, then
discreetly moved on, and as he did so his eyes saw

an unusual thing, the form of a great, gaunt, hungry *dog*, *alone* in the wild.

An event happened late this winter that brought the worst trouble to Shag. One afternoon the ever alert and keen-eyed Jess Forrester was riding slowly along a little valley by the Big Aspen River, when he pulled his horse up with a jerk and looked with wide eyes through a cut in a long ridge. Jess had been searching for his outlaw mare, a fine chestnut sorrel called Old Moll, and now he saw her, but saw her only for a moment as she ran at breakneck speed past a cut in the ridge, a big dog running behind her with all his power. It was Shag.

Quick as the rush past the cut had been, Jess drew his revolver and fired, then spurred for the cut. The chestnut mare was soon far down the ridges, and she and the dog behind her disappeared. Shag was now running in terror. The bullet fired at him had cut a flesh wound in his hip. Jess Forrester stormed and fumed. He supposed that he had caught Shag in a desperate attempt to bring down the mare. He did not know that the furious burst of speed had come because both the mare and the dog had seen him, and that of late they had formed a strange companionship in the wild.

Jess did know that for Old Moll, the outlaw, to see a mounted man was to run like the wildest of wild horses. And now it seemed that Shag had

*c

turned to a wolf-dog of the most vicious and dangerous type.

Jess spurred his horse hard along the base of the ridges, but his mount at a dead run was no match for Old Moll of thoroughbred stock. In the distance she had vanished, and so had the dog.

Jess pulled up at the edge of a wild country of ravines and deep gorges with thick-set pine-woods covering all the slopes and allowed his puffing horse to stand. High above the scene an eagle hung poised on silent wings, and a deep stillness reigned, save for the laboured breathing of Jess Forrester's heaving, sweating horse. It was getting late; already the dusk of evening was gathering, and Jess at last turned homeward to report what he had seen.

In view of the singular companionship that had grown up between Shag and this unsociable outlaw mare some mention of her is here necessary. In colour she was, as has been described, a chestnut sorrel. Of thoroughbred stock, she could outrun any horse on the range. For more than two years she had run wild, and when Jess Forrester with his men tried to get around her to bring her in, the wily mare was always on guard. Just when Jess believed he was circumventing her he would get only a glimpse of her, as with flying mane and tail she went thundering away through canyon or valley. And Old Moll also had proved too swift and clever

SHE CAME UP TO HIM

for wolves. Oddly enough, although this wild outlaw was seldom seen within a mile of the other
horses, she formed a strange companionship with
the outcast, lonely dog.

It was Shag who brought it about. Seeing her
so often alone in the wild as he did, and feeling that
she, like himself, was not of the wild, but, also like
himself, seemed by nature to belong to men, he
first got to standing and looking at her in a peaceful,
quiet manner. The mare, after looking at him for
a little, knew he was not a wolf, and she came to
be pleased when he was near. After a time Shag
would lie down not far from her, and at last quite
near to her, when they would rest long hours
together. Old Moll was always ready to run the
instant a horseman was sighted. And Shag, too,
had now become afraid of men. He was ready to
get quickly out of sight with Old Moll.

The ever alert Old Moll had seen Jess Forrester
before he saw her. That was why he saw her
running when he fired the shot; but she knew
nothing of what that meant to Shag, and when she
and Shag at last stopped running, after having
penetrated far into the region, she could not understand the little cries of Shag. She came up to him
and whinnied low, but he seemed to have forgotten
her for the time. The physical pain of the wound
would have been nothing; he had had worse from

the wolves and paid little attention to them, because wolves were his natural enemies. But Shag couldn't feel that way toward men. He longed for them— as friends.

Six days now passed in which Shag's fear of men grew in him, but in all this he did not fear Tom Glen. He only believed Tom did not want him. And then one night an overwhelming desire came over Shag to try for his home once more.

In the far distant region of the Rim Rock, Shag one morning took leave of Old Moll, and started away toward the home of Tom Glen. As he moved farther to the south he became more and more alert, watching for men as a wolf would watch for them, knowing now as well as a hunted wolf would know that men can kill a great distance away.

Shag travelled watchfully all that day and again the next, until at last he was in the heart of the Tom Glen country, and still he travelled, until one moonlight night from a high hill he could see the place of Tom Glen. All night, in spite of the chill, Shag by turns sat down and walked about on the hill and looked; and he wanted desperately to go down to the silent ranch-house, but the memory of the lashing Tom had given him made him afraid. Before daybreak, his head hanging in dejection, Shag started away toward the distant region of the Rim Rock and travelled on, back toward the place where he had left his odd companion—Old Outlaw Moll.

Again as he travelled Shag became uneasy and alert. That day, about noon, while he was loping along a valley, watching now constantly, Jess Forrester and a dozen of his men loomed suddenly on a hill to the rear. With wild yells Jess and the men rode hard after the dog. Fortunately for Shag he was out of range. Although men fired at him, the bullets kicked up the sand and gravel well behind him, and Shag swiftly out-distanced his pursuers. When he reached the cover of a long belt of timber he still ran with all his power for a great distance, and so eluded them completely.

On and on Shag moved, loping, trotting, panting, toward the place Old Moll herself had chosen. At last he saw her and came up. And when the cold, dark night came they moved in among some sheltering trees and laid themselves down very close together.

CHAPTER VIII

NEWS FROM THE RIM ROCK

IT was just sunrise.

'What do you suppose is the latest about Shag?' said Jim Williams as he pulled up his puffing horse beside that of young Len Pitts on the West Valley of the Glen Range.

'What?'—young Pitts shot the word out, all attention.

'The men over on the Rim Rock say Shag's running with a small pack of timber wolves, helping them to kill horses. Cow-puncher over there by the name of Hawkins says he saw the yellow lobo running a bunch of wild horses, and once he *thought* he saw Shag running some range horses, although he told me himself he couldn't be *positive* it was Shag. The talk is,' Jim went on, 'that another cowboy was coming across the valley pretty late in the moonlight, and that while he couldn't swear it was Shag, yet he feels certain it *was* him and not the yellow lobo, as the animal he saw was too rangy for the wolf. He says he knows it must have been Shag, because there is no other wolf or dog as big as either of these.'

'And all that in the dim moonlight,' said Len Pitts. 'I don't believe it! I'll ride right over there and see what I can find out!'

'And I'll hunt up Tom and tell him,' said Williams. 'This talk is going to make it dangerous for Shag.'

When late evening came and Len Pitts came riding home Tom Glen was awaiting him.

'Just as I expected,' Len said, pulling the saddle from his sweating horse. 'It's the old story of give a dog a bad name. The men out there believe Shag is running with the wolves, but not one has actually seen him for certain. You know Jess Forrester *thought* Shag was trying to bring down Old Moll, and *that* makes the men believe anything— and makes it awful dangerous for Shag. If we could only get hold of him!'

For a time no one reported seeing Shag. Many were the guesses concerning him. Some said he had likely gone into the far North-West, into the wilds near the Canyon River, to hunt with the wolves; but others thought he might be still hovering around the mountains of the Sweet Briar region or those along the Big Aspen River, hiding by day with the wolves and coming out at night to attack cattle and horses. All this time, however, the days passed and he was not once seen. And while big tracks were in evidence now and then, there was no certain way of telling whether they were those of Shag or the yellow lobo. Shag was as big as the lobo, and his track might easily have been mistaken for that of the big wolf.

As the weeks went by and Old Moll was not seen by any man, the range men generally frowned and profoundly believed Shag was most guilty.

In all this, however, Tom Glen faced every man, and with his steel-blue eyes looking squarely into theirs he defended Shag. 'He's guilty of nothing until you have proof of it,' said Glen to them. 'And I'll confess this, that I am to blame and I alone, because Shag's not at this hour with me in the only home he ever knew.'

So the relations between Tom Glen and the range men became a little strained, though there was honour among them all. They knew to a man that if damage was proved against Shag, Tom Glen would pay for it, although as yet he had not said so. That, however, would come.

CHAPTER IX

THE FIGHT WITH THE LOBO

SPRING came and passed. The long summer days went slowly by. The haze of autumn again hung silent on hill and valley. Little plains that had been covered with lovely green now lay in the grey of death from the frost-blighting nights. Here and there in lonely ravines the gold and crimson leaves of the aspen and cotton-wood lay strewn on the ground along the little streams. And far and near a sober stillness lay on the land.

Again the cold of December came.

In all these months Shag was never seen save once. Late one cold winter evening young Len Pitts, far from the ranch, field-glasses to his eyes, saw far up on Baldy Mountain, many miles to the north, the form of Shag. He stood for a little, thin, ill-looking, the spirit of misery, against a background of frozen white, and while Len Pitts looked, vanished in the gloom of the falling winter night.

Honest but terribly mistaken men had for weeks hunted Shag to kill him. But after the second shots were fired at him Shag left their range. Then

Tom Glen made a truce for Shag by offering to pay three times any damage the dog did. But all that Shag knew was that there was danger for him in the region he had known as home. Long hours by day and longer hours by night Shag lay near Old Moll, living on, yet with no interest in life. And as the bitter, lonely days went by his heart never once deserted Tom Glen, but, on the contrary, the loneliness and sorrow bore down the heavier upon him.

The ever alert and wily Old Moll held to the lowlands, where in the mornings she fed nervously on the withered grasses near gorge and canyon and sometimes on the green buds of the trees. Shag, moving away to hunt his own food in the wild, was never away from her long at any one time, and many times in his hunting he would stop suddenly on a hill-top and look down in a valley to make sure his companion was there.

One bitter cold day in December Shag came upon the trail of the yellow wolf. Shag had scented food, and coming at a run eagerly toward it, did not see danger until too late. He plunged through some tall, dead grass, and leaped down a low embankment almost upon the lobo, which was crunching the bones of a horse's carcass.

Shag and the wolf whirled on the instant. Deadly fiery eyes met deadly fiery eyes as the lobo, his lips curled back, slowly circled for an opening. The lobo struck, but Shag met him and fang clashed fang. Again they both struck and leaped back, each with a shoulder slashed. Again the slow, deadly circling of the lobo and again Shag faced him, not only faced him but edged a little nearer, then made a lightning strike and ripped the lobo's shoulder.

At this moment there sounded on the hill-top to the south the wild howl of another timber wolf. Shag knew that here was another enemy. Slowly he retreated, snarling. The lobo did not follow. A little farther on Shag looked back. The lobo and the other wolf were at the carcass, where they were feeding and snarling.

Shag circled back to Old Moll, who had scented the wolves, and her eyes were ablaze with fear and anger. She started away rapidly, Shag loping beside her. After travelling for miles they turned by common instinct into some low ground with a frozen swale and many little bushes, tall, withered grasses, and scattering trees along the margins.

Shag's shoulder stung him and made him restless. Once Old Moll came up, looked at him, put her nose rather close, then went on with her feeding on the withered grass.

Although the day was cold it was clear, and after a time Shag curled up beside a bush and tried to

forget his pain. He closed his eyes as the winter
sun shone down upon him, but did not sleep. A
great danger in the yellow beast threatened, and
Shag knew it. He did not know why the lobo had
travelled here. He only knew it was so. The
truth was that the lobo had been hunted so hard
on the Tamarack, and food in this bitter winter
had become so scarce, that he had travelled away
from his many hunters and had come into a region
where there was but one man, the trapper, old
Bob McKee. McKee knew already that this wily
brute was now in this vicinity. He had twice seen
him, although he had no chance for a shot, and
Bob had set out in the hills a wolf trap which he
viewed each morning from a distance so that no
man-scent might taint the place.

Likewise old Bob had learned from a passing
trapper all the late news about Shag, and McKee
believed in Shag the more because Tom Glen
believed.

As Shag lay and shivered, the hours passed and
the shadows of evening came on. He now and then
raised his head, cocked up his ears, and looked and
sniffed the air for signs of the enemy—and Shag
was still troubled. Now the place where Shag lay,
and likewise the thickets behind which Old Moll
pulled at the withered grass, concealed them wholly
from the north, and if it had not been for the sharp

eyes of Old Moll, Bob McKee might have come up very close.

All at once several things happened. Old Moll snorted wildly and started at a run for the woods. Shag raced after her. Old Bob, on his way to his hut, fired through the shadows at what he was positive was the lobo wolf, missed, then stood with mouth and eyes open—in amazement at what he knew to be Old Moll—and Shag! Shag was ahead of Old Moll, running for his life, and she followed hard behind, followed and turned *with* him when he circled a little to the west and raced into the woods.

Old Bob's mouth opened and closed a number of times as if he were about to speak, then he said: 'Now think of that! No matter what Jess Forrester saw, he didn't see that Shag dog trying to bring down Old Moll. Jess made an awful mistake. Why, Old Moll wouldn't leave him! It's awful— the whole thing. And here *I've* shot at him! No chance now for *me* ever to get close to him. To think of it—I was trying to *kill* him, but I missed— clear—thunder! I *hope* I ain't hurt him.'

Old Bob stood for a time revolving over in his mind what was best to do. Here was Shag away out here. Tom Glen had tried to get him, but the men hunting Shag had frightened him terribly. All of this old Bob knew. It would be best, then, to

OLD MOLL . . . STARTED AT A RUN FOR THE WOODS

try to get word to Tom Glen. This would mean a big loss to McKee in leaving his traps.

McKee stood for a time looking at the dark woods where Shag had vanished. He believed the dog was fearfully poor.

'I'd throw some food out for him near the cabin,' McKee said, 'but he'd be afraid to come up—now. No, he'll run from me now as he'd run from death. Glen was over once last winter. Maybe he'll take a notion to come over again soon. If Tom don't come I'll just leave things here and travel and tell him.'

Bob turned, and had almost reached his cabin, when he stopped all at once, a look of deep concern in his eyes. He looked toward the west. It was getting dark. 'It's too late to go out to that wolf trap to-night,' he said, 'it's way off to the north anyway. Don't look like Shag would get caught in it to-night. I hate to be away out there in the night. If that yellow lobo'd see me, why I know he'd tackle me if he could get the least drop on me. No, I don't think Shag's in any danger of that just for to-night. I'll get up bright and early though and take up that wolf trap. It *would* be dangerous now to leave it there as before. But I won't. I'll take it up bright and early in the morning.'

CHAPTER X

THE TRAP

THAT night in the shelter of a ravine in the hills Shag and Old Moll stopped. They were both afraid to remain in the forest, and the ravine gave shelter from the driving wind. Old Moll was a veteran at wresting her food from a winter-blasted land. She was thin, to be sure, but wiry and tough as a pine knot. She knew how to forage for green buds and dead grass, and to paw down through the snow for the cured buffalo grass beneath. But Shag was not so fortunate, and he could find no rest here. Hunger gnawed and at last drove him forth into the open. There was not a cloud in the sky when he started, but the stars shone dimly and the wind roared and hissed across hills and draws. Shag hunted on for several miles, but found nothing except the sting of the biting wind as it blew in a fine spray from the drifts. A ravine loomed before him. He slowed his pace and cautiously approached the gorge.

Near the edge of the wood a cotton-tail started up out of the snow and Shag rushed frantically for it. His only reward was a bit of fur snatched from its tail as it raced over the snow, then down the ravine. The rabbit ran easily and lightly, but Shag broke through the snow crust as he ran and fell headlong down the ravine. The game vanished.

Shag, for a little, lay panting in the bottom of the ravine. Then he got up, and started down the gorge hunting for food, his burning eyes searching for any dark thing that might move on the snow. Farther down in the ravine bed he started up a covey of quail. They were startled, but only mocked him as he followed them. A little farther down they alighted, but at his approach they started up again and flew away. He was well aware that he could not succeed in stalking them, but as fear of death makes a drowning man grasp at a bobbing cork, so hunger drove him after them. But this time the covey left the gorge, and flew away over the hill to the east. Shag looked after them longingly as they soared upward in the starlit sky. He took a pace forward in some bushes, and then suddenly leaped into the air and snapped viciously at a great horned owl that had swung low, like a shadow, over him. The owl, frightened at his unexpected presence, flapped its silent wings and bore upward. For another hour Shag roamed this ravine, seeing nothing on the wastes of snow, and hearing nothing but the dismal creaking of the frozen branches of the tall, dark trees. He struggled up the long, steep side of the gorge, and again made for the open. As he moved along he sniffed the wind and stopped to listen. His slashed shoulder was stiff from frozen blood, and it annoyed him.

Hours passed as Shag wandered across valleys and over hills, meeting not a single living thing. But there was no seeking shelter or rest. His hunger was now torturing him. He hunted on through the shelter of another small gorge, and came out on the level land above them. No sooner had he come up out of the ravine than he scented meat!

The scent was borne down on the stinging north wind, and Shag, desperate to get it quickly, raced madly toward the scent in the teeth of the gale. Down a snow-clad hill and into a little valley, near a clump of small pines, he found what he was seeking. Hunger made it hard for him to hold himself back from rushing directly up and seizing the meat. But, in spite of his great hunger, he hesitated, for he scented something besides meat. It was the trail of the beast he so much dreaded— the huge yellow wolf. The trail of the wolf was very recent, and it led in a complete circle around the meat, but not *up to it*. And the man-scent that Shag now dreaded was there. Shag hesitated. He sniffed around the circular trail of the wolf

twice. Why had not the wolf eaten the meat?
Shag's fear was not so definite as that of the trap-
wise wolf. His tongue hung low as he walked
nearer; he scented iron now, but it held no meaning
of fear for him.

In view of what happened here this place must
be described. The meat lay on a little patch of
level ground, a few feet from a sharp 'jump-off'
about ten feet high. A small pine-tree stood almost
at the edge of this cliff, and near by stood the burned
stump of another pine. It was this little pine and
the near-by stump that were to play, as it proved,
such a strange part in a game of life and death here
that night.

Shag started directly toward the meat, but
stopped short, for the still, small voice of caution
whispered: 'Beware! Something wrong here!' To
satisfy this a bit he trotted around near the 'jump-
off', and approached the food from that direction.
He took one cautious step forward, then another,
looking quickly on all sides of him in the darkness,
until, reaching out, he seized the food. It would
not come, and he braced his legs and pulled on the
frozen meat. He wanted to take it away because
the lobo's scent was so strong there. He moved
his feet again as he pulled. There came a dull
thump—his foot was fast in the grip of two iron
jaws. He leaped, was jerked back, and the trap

bit in just above his hind foot. But the bone in
Shag's leg was strong. The trap jaws did not
break it.

The trap, close to the cliff, was attached to a
chain, six feet long. Shag lurched desperately in
every direction except toward the cliff; that way
he sensed a terrible thing. If he sprang over the
cliff it could only result in his dangling in mid-
air, helpless and in fearful pain.

He struggled for freedom until his heart beat
hard and fast, then he lay down, panting hard for
breath. Horror at being caught and held fast by
the trap was worse than the pain in his foot. He
panted as if he had run a race on a hot day. His
ears, by turns, stood up, then flattened down on
his head. When the steel jaws first gripped him he
bit them savagely, but he tried that only once.
He knew he could not use his fangs to free himself.
Nothing came of it, and once more he lay down
exhausted, panting and quivering from head to foot.
In the clear night a cold winter moon was up and
looked down on the scene. A biting north wind
swept snow and frost in Shag's face, and when he
put out his tongue the frost bit it like fire. Looking
helplessly back at his trapped foot, he panted a
little, drew in his tongue to avoid the piercing sting,
and panted again. The night grew steadily colder,
and sharp gusts of wind, difficult to stand against,

buffeted Shag mercilessly when he got to his feet. He knew no other way than to struggle against death until it should overcome him.

A sharp stinging sensation in his nose, which steadily grew worse, made it difficult for him to breathe, and with each effort to free himself he grew weaker. He might have worked his body around and gnawed off the trapped foot. Not want of courage kept him from doing so, but a dogged determination to be free—free and whole—and again able to battle for life.

Having renewed the struggle again and again, he at last lay down more dead than alive. Suddenly he drew in his tongue, and a fear shot through and through him like fire. He sprang up and stood, head erect, listening intently. He forgot the pain in his foot, and the bitter, cutting wind. He forgot everything but the fear of the big lobo wolf. Shag heard him coming directly up from the south with a deep, wild howl. There was not the least doubt that this enemy had scented him, that he had found his trail, and was now racing directly in the teeth of the wind with the intention of devouring him.

Maddened with fear at being thus helplessly trapped, Shag turned toward what had seemed an impossible way of escape. He had tried every other way—now he would try the last and most dangerous way out of his difficulty. In a wild

HE PLUNGED OVER THE EDGE

frenzy of fear he leaped with all his might out
and over the cliff.

As he plunged over the edge of the steep the trap
caught between the pine and the stump in such a
way that both springs were jammed hard, and the
shock of Shag's weight jerked his foot free.

He tumbled in a heap on the snow below, and in
an instant was up and running with all the speed
he could muster with the stiffened foot. The pain
of putting the hurt foot to the ground was nothing
to him now, but the foot hindered him.

He tried, however, to make up for the loss of
speed by clever dodging, for the wild, deep howl of
the huge lobo sounded nearer. Shag was weak.
He dreaded the encounter now.

He ran down the gorge for a short distance, then
struggled up the side to the open land above,
doubling back to the south, and so had the wind
in his favour. But the lobo struck the hot trail
and raced down the gorge.   When Shag again turned
he realized the beast was almost upon him and,
being unfamiliar with his surroundings, he could
not pick the best direction to escape.

On came the big lobo like a demon, hunger giving
him greater speed. Again Shag rushed down the
side of a small draw and across to the opposite
side. Now the lobo was directly opposite him.
Shag plunged away, with no particular plan of

escape, but with a fiery desire now to give battle, yet fearful he might have to fight more than one foe.

He rushed up a turn in the draw, where a stream bed made a sharp curve to the right. Here he ran for the open, coming out on a wide stretch of level land. Afraid to turn back, he again headed across the snow, running blindly on, knowing his enemy was drawing nearer and nearer to him, and yet having no power to increase his speed, for his foot troubled him constantly. Then the dark woods of a creek loomed just ahead.

Suddenly what Shag had feared most during his short life happened—the big wolf was upon him. Shag whirled in time to evade the first rush, then faced his enemy with bared fangs. The big wolf rushed in and slashed once. A new fire suddenly shot through Shag. Although somewhat lighter in weight than his enemy, a ferocious strength arose within him. Forgotten was the pain in his foot.

Now it happened that this dangerous beast, sensing he was to satisfy his long hunger, was not aware of a small log cabin in a thick-set pine timber close by. Shag, in his desperate situation, had no thought of a human being so near and, if he had, perhaps would have been only the more frightened. But it was at that still hour, far in the night, when so many tragedies of the wild happen, that Bob McKee awakened in his cabin at the head of Little

D

Pine Creek. At first he heard, as he thought, the sounds of two tremendous grey wolves in mortal combat. He got up quickly and, rifle in hand, hurried out under the trees to look. In an instant the dramatic battle was before him, and McKee jerked his rifle to his shoulder, but the next instant he dropped his gun to his side. It flashed in his brain that he heard the wild snarls of a dog. What other dog could there be here but Shag! All this in a flash.

Old Bob now ran out, shouting the name of Shag. He saw two forms run in opposite directions, one uttering a cry of fear, and in the moonlight he saw the great white head. Now he knew it was Shag. On the instant McKee whirled and fired at the other silent, running form, but missed it in the shadowy night.

'Shag! Shag! Come, Shag!' Bob shouted in the cold night, but only the sullen roar and the hissing of the wind broke the silence. 'Poor Shag—I know that's him,' moaned Bob. 'He and the lobo—both awful big—I wonder how it would have come out? I'll look at the place in the morning, and as soon as it's light I'll go over and take up that wolf trap.'

CHAPTER XI

CONSPIRATORS

THE next morning at daybreak Bob McKee was out at the scene of conflict. No snow or sleet had fallen during the later hours of the night, and Bob, with his keen grey eyes, saw the story in the tracks.

'It sure was Shag fighting the lobo,' he said, straightening up, 'and my shot at that wolf only made Shag think I was shooting at him again. This is awful for him — his right hind foot shows blood in the track—reckon the lobo got him there. I 'll hurry over and take up that wolf trap.'

When McKee came up to the trap a little later he examined the place and the trap critically. Finally, he held the trap in his hands. 'Now, ain't that a shame!' he exclaimed; 'I *did* ketch Shag after all—that 's what made red show in his track. The lobo come up—Shag jumped, trap and all, over the cliff and jerked loose.'

It was three o'clock that afternoon when Bob McKee walked up on a ridge above his log hut. He could scarcely believe his eyes, yet it was so— the tall, six-foot form of Tom Glen stood just out in the clearing, looking down on the dog and wolf tracks. Old Bob hurried down to meet him.

'Tom!' old Bob burst out, 'I'd rather see you than any man alive!' And while McKee rattled off all he knew about Shag, Tom Glen stood intently listening. He made only brief comment, after his manner: 'Bob, I've been trying so long to get him—I've known from the first that something was wrong with Jess's story—Jess is truthful—but I knew there was some mistake'.

The two men stood and talked for a little time, when old Bob said: 'Tom, after all that's happened you'll never get up to him again unless you somehow trap him, and let him see that you really want him'. And at this the old trapper's mind hit on a scheme.

'I tell you!' he burst forth; 'Shag's starving. We'll fix up the old bear-trap hut up yonder on the hill. I never ketched a dog that way, but maybe it can be done. It won't hurt him if you can ketch him that way, and you're the man to fix it. If Shag gets the scent of you, and you only, around that place, I have a notion you may turn the trick, for he'll be curious. It won't take a great while to fix the old trap, and I'll tell you how to do it. Come in the shack, Tom. I'll tell you *exactly* how to do it. No bears around here any more, and it's not likely the lobo would go in, but if Shag gets the scent of you and meat too, well, unless I don't know him at all, he's going to be mighty curious, and when the darkness comes he'll investigate.'

The two men went into the cabin. Old Bob pointed to the bear trap that was plainly visible high up on the sparsely wooded slope to the west. It was a small, completely covered enclosure, made like a hut, save that the posts had been set deep in the ground, and it was very strongly made.

In a short time old Bob had explained his plans, and a little later Glen, an axe on his shoulder, a rawhide lariat on one arm, and a good-sized piece of frozen beef under the other, started up to the old bear trap. When this trap had been made, years before, a tall tree had stood but a few feet from the door. One night a violent wind blew across the mountain, uprooting this tree and leaving a great hole in its place. When Tom came up he surveyed the hole casually, and merely noted at the time that an animal, to walk into the trap, must go round the hole to get into the hut.

Tom Glen set to work. When the bear trap had been made by Bob McKee he had fixed a swinging door in such a manner that when the bait, inside on a rope, was pulled, the door slammed shut from the inside and a heavy wooden pin dropped in place on the inside of the door. A black bear was thus

caught ten years before, and strive as he would
against the door, he had only pushed it the harder
against the stout frame. Tom examined the pin;
it was still good. 'The pin will hold,' he mused,
'unless Shag, after being caught, should lift it up
with his teeth; but that would be very hard, even
if he tried it.'

Tom worked for a long time on the door. Using
three iron rings taken from trap chains, he attached
the rawhide lariat rope to the door in such a way
that when the suspended meat was pulled down the
door would slam shut and the wooden pin drop in
its place perfectly. Then Glen stepped outside,
closed the door and pulled the rope from the outside;
the arrangement instantly lifted the wooden pin
inside, thus letting the door swing open.

'Fine!' said Glen, and he looked at the long piece
of rope hanging out and lying on the snow. At
first he was minded to cut the rope up short, but a
cowman dislikes to spoil a good rawhide rope.
The extra length would do no harm, Tom thought,
so let it remain. Then, after dragging the meat
over a long and toilsome trail, he returned, still
dragging it, and fixed the trap and the bait in
readiness for the venture.

By this time night was coming on, and it was
dark when Tom Glen got back to the cabin of Bob
McKee. The day had been cold, but clear, and

the night was also clear when Glen got back to the cabin.

The two men finished supper; then Bob threw more wood on the fire, and they set themselves down by the warming blaze to speculate on what would happen out on the cold mountain-side. An hour went by and another, and still another, then McKee said: 'Tom, I 'm awful sleepy'.

'You go to bed, Bob,' said Tom Glen, 'I don't feel sleepy.'

McKee lay down and was soon sound asleep.

On this bitter cold night, as the time passed, the moon came up and anything that moved might be seen on the open wastes. About ten o'clock the wind arose, and hissed and moaned around the little cabin where old Bob lay peacefully sleeping. Tom Glen, however, was up, sitting on a bench, wide awake. Harder and harder the gale swept on, but all was still in the little hut. Only once old Bob McKee moved a little in his sleep, when he dreamed Shag was in the trap and it seemed that something awful had happened to Tom Glen. The fire burned on, and there was only the flicker of the flames in the fire-place and the moaning of the wind as it searched every nook and crevice to lash and sting everything that breathed.

CHAPTER XII

FIGHTERS IN ACTION

IT was well along in the night when Shag, after trying in vain to rest, got to his feet. He was standing near Old Moll in the shelter of some pines at the upper end of the narrow valley. Below them this valley had only a few trees here and there, and these stood out dark and dismal from the deep snow that covered the ground.

The night was so cold that with all his soul Shag disliked to move out in the cutting wind, but there was no other way. Gnawing hunger made it impossible for him to stay where he was. He had hunted all day for food and found only a few of the bones left from a mink carcass that some wild thing had eaten. Shag groaned a little at the necessity of it all, then started out in the gloom of the night, limping on his injured foot.

In a little time he was at the outer edge of the bushes skirting the lower part of the valley. At the same instant the delicious scent of meat met his nose. He pushed out his long neck and sniffed eagerly, then started at a lope in the direction of the scent. All at once he struck the trail and away he ran, his nose close to the snow over which the precious food had passed. Skirting the edge of the valley for half a mile at a limping run, he plunged around a clump of bushes and headed up the slope. With the scent of the meat another smell came to Shag, and, starving though he was, this other scent thrilled him and made him utter low sounds of mingled joy and fear. He knew the man who had made that trail.

When Shag started up the slope he stopped often and looked up quickly. He was both glad and afraid and terribly hungry. Then he found where the meat was, and found it in a place which seemed to him suspicious. It was suspicious because the man-smell was there. While he was not much afraid of this particular man, still, other men might have had a part in this. Shag circled the little log shack three times, sniffing at the logs, and finally he came close to the door, his muscles ready for a backward spring. At last he stood within, looking up in the darkness. The smell was so pungent that the saliva drooled down from his great jaws. But now he had learned to be wary, and he still hesitated. He stepped quickly back to the doorway and looked out into the moonlight. The wind hissed ceaselessly over the lonely mountain. Flurries of snow, whipped up by the wind here and there, rushed on with a

*D

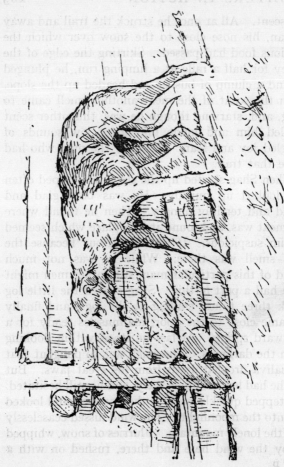

SNIFFING AT THE LOGS

sighing sound; then the wind died down to a low, sullen roar. Shag was still suspicious. He again walked around the outside of the crude hut, sniffing and whining in his eagerness to get at the life-giving food, yet afraid—afraid because of what had happened to him in the wolf trap. There was nothing like that—nothing at all like it, yet he was afraid. Shag walked to the door again, and for some time he stood, ears cocked up, turning his head now on this side, now on that, trying to fathom the mystery of this meat that he knew was hanging down from the top of the little hut. He moved inside.

Now he looked directly up at the food. He could not see it, but the smell was overwhelmingly good. Suddenly he heard a sound. Leaping back to the door, he listened. It was the wild, weird howl of a big timber wolf, borne down on the north wind. It seemed far away, but Shag sensed the truth. It was the yellow lobo on the trail of the meat. The thing to do then was to get the meat instantly and eat it quickly! Shag stood on his hind feet, put his forepaws on the logs, seized the meat and jerked down hard.

Instantly there came a thump behind him; the old door slammed shut and the wooden pin fell true to its place. Shag was a prisoner. At first he leaped for the door, but finding it shut, and being so famished, he tore at the meat and gulped it down. Then he began frantic efforts to get out. Time after time he stood up with his forepaws on the crude door and sank his teeth into the stout wood. As he did this he cried in his fear. The situation made him every moment more afraid, and he began to imagine that the men who on the range had tried to do away with him would come and destroy him. Shag had no way of knowing how the door was held shut, and it was only chance that in biting at the wooden door his fangs sank in the wooden pin and moved it—moved it so that it held by only half an inch. Again and again he sank his teeth into the door and once again they grazed the bar, but in such a way that it was not moved either up or down. The bar held, yet only by that little. At last he dropped down panting.

After resting a little he did a strange thing. Knowing that he was now a hopeless prisoner, and that men could destroy him at their will, he sat up, and pointing his nose upward uttered a prolonged, mournful howl. Again the howl went out through the crude shack and down the lonely mountain. It was a howl that, like the strange carrying power of a dog's bark, arose above the hissing and roaring of the wind and swept down and across the valley to the slope beyond—the howl of a good dog whose soul was in the depths of despair—his howl of death.

A PROLONGED, MOURNFUL HOWL

But human ears heard. Down to the log hut
where Tom Glen sat wide awake the lonely howl
carried. Instantly Glen's eyes opened wide. The
howl seemed to be somewhat muffled.

'I got him!' Glen said, under his breath. 'I'll
hurry up there and see—no use to wake up Bob.'
Quickly Glen put on his heavy outer clothing and
slipped quietly out into the night. On and up the
slope he moved. Again came the long, mournful
howl, when Tom Glen was half-way up the slope;
after that he heard nothing more. Glen covered
half the remaining distance and stopped a moment,
saying to himself: 'Now, I wonder if I've been a
fool. Maybe he was just *behind* the trap. But I
can soon tell'.

On and up came the gentle 'tramp, tramp' of
Glen's boots on the frozen snow. Presently he
stood beside the door of the trap. It was shut.
Glen put his ear to the door and listened. Within
was absolute silence; still he listened, his mouth a
little open, the better to hear the faintest sound,
but only the constant hissing of the wind broke the
stillness. Tom stood for a moment considering.
He called softly the name of Shag, but still there
was no sound within. He knew that probably
Shag was now afraid of him. And why not? The
dog had been through so much; he had been so
desperately frightened, and he must know that he

had been tricked into this prison. Glen decided
that it would not be wise to try to get his hands on
Shag in the darkness. At the first opening of the
door he might rush out and escape. It would be
better to hold him there until daylight came, when
a perfect understanding might be had between
them. And now, looking about to make it more
certain that Shag would not by some chance raise
the wooden pin inside high enough to get out,
Glen's eyes fell upon something that he believed
would help in holding the pin more secure. This
was a long, heavy stone, twice as long as broad.
'Just the thing,' Glen thought, 'to lean against the
door so that the wooden pin inside will be pressed
harder against its cleat.' He stooped over the
stone and began to work it out of the frozen snow
by pulling up the free end.

As Glen did this the form of a huge yellow wolf
passed through the shadows just behind and above
him. With burning eyes he stood behind a small
bush watching, and as Tom pulled again at the
rock the giant wolf, now deadly from his long
hunger, stole swiftly nearer the unsuspecting man.
The lobo also had struck the trail of the meat, and
followed it, only to find the being he most feared
and hated—a man. The lobo would not have thus
slunk upon any animal of the wild. He would have
run on and on and on, howling on the trail, and at

last rushing openly upon his game. But the man,
alive and alert, was deadly, and so the beast used
caution here. Let the man so much as fall to the
ground or show any sign of helplessness and it
would be over! Softly the great, gaunt beast slunk
from one granite rock to another; and then a scent
struck his nose with great force—the scent of a dog.
Even at this the lobo only lay low to the snow in
the shadow of the rocks. His instinct told him the
dog was in the shack, but something was wrong,
for the dog made no noise.

The night was intensely cold, and Glen, after
getting the stone nearly to the door, stopped,
anxious to get some response from within. 'Shag!
Shag! Don't you know me?' And then he thrilled
as a faint whine sounded within. He was there!
But Tom thought he must be careful. If he opened
the door in the darkness wide enough to go in,
Shag might still rush out. Glen had worked the
stone nearly to the door; now he would complete
his work. He stooped down over the big stone.
It was very heavy, and he started to move it again
by raising one end. He had lifted the end of the
stone half-way up, when one of his feet encountered
the rawhide rope, dangling on the ground, that was
fixed to open the door from the outside. The rope,
unnoticed, had lain curled on the snow. Glen,
feeling the rope around his ankle, and knowing at

once what it was, kicked out his foot to free it
from the rope. At this an appalling thing happened.
Glen's other foot slipped on the sleet at the edge of
the hole, and he fell heavily on his side, clutching
at the up-ended stone before he could think, and so
bringing it tumbling down upon his right leg with
all but crushing force. He had no sooner felt the
shock of this than he was horrified to see the flash
of a huge form above the hole, and the giant lobo
stood, slightly crouching, snarling and looking down
upon him.

Instinct made the beast understand that the
fallen man was helpless. This was a man, to be
sure, but he was down! Tom Glen shouted with
all his might to frighten the lobo, and he called for
Shag: 'Take him, Shag!' never thinking it possible
the dog could get out, yet hoping that if Shag snarled
or growled the lobo might be held off until Glen
could work himself free. Yet, when he heaved
again, he knew the crushing weight would hold.

The lobo took three steps down the slope of the
hole. Tom Glen heard Shag whining now and
frantically gnawing at the door. Glen, desperate
to do something, snatched at the snow to throw it
into the wolf's face, when his hand encountered the
long piece of rawhide rope. In kicking this rope
from his feet he had not only caused his fall, but
also had kicked the free end of the rope down with

him. A wild hope came to Glen. On the instant he seized the rope and pulled it hard. He felt the wooden pin inside give instantly, and he let loose the rope so that the door might swing in.

In the moonlight there was a sudden rush, the flash of another great body, and Shag shot out and struck the lobo—crashed against him with such violence that they both went down in the hole fighting. The awful fight was on top of the man. Glen jerked his face over and downward, clutched the back of his neck with both hands. He felt the skin being scratched from the backs of his hands. Twice great toe-nails ripped through his scalp and the blood ran. Once a huge head was pressed hard against his own, driving his head into the sleet and snow until he was almost suffocated. Now a great weight was resting on him with only slight movements and he could scarcely get his breath. Then came a sob and a groan, and the long-trailing cry of a dog, but it came strangely muffled to Tom Glen, for consciousness had left him.

It could not have been for long. He came to himself, frightened when he turned to find a huge, furry beast across him. It was the yellow lobo—dead! Glen heaved and was barely able to hurl the thing off. 'Shag! Shag!' Glen called. At that moment he heard sounds of crunching snow, and old Bob McKee loomed above him.

Astonished, McKee leaped down, lifted and grunted, and got the rock off. Then he dragged Tom up to the level ground. The leg was not broken. Tom got to his feet and held to Bob from sheer weakness, while telling him what had happened. 'And Shag is gone—afraid of *me*!' Tom groaned.

'But I was the one that frightened him, Tom,' Bob put in. 'When I woke up and saw you gone I got out in a hurry with a gun, thinking you had heard something up here. I got up close enough to see Shag pretty plain. He was standing with his head down, making little uneasy sounds all to himself. He had killed the wolf, and you were so still there. I guess that's why he didn't see or hear me sooner. He had his whole mind on you. But the minute he saw me he ran with a cry—I'll never forget it, Tom. It wasn't just because he was afraid, although that was a lot of it. But come on now down to the fire. Your hands are badly cut. I'll drag the lobo down as we go.'

There was no sleep for either of the men that night. McKee put dressings on Tom's hands. They sat up and looked at the dead lobo—and waited. Was Shag himself badly hurt, even mortally wounded? This might well be, and he might have been bleeding dangerously when he managed to run at the sight of Bob McKee.

Tom Glen drank some hot tea, then paced the floor.
Dawn came, with a cloudy sky and a sullen wind.
As soon as it was light enough to see, both men
started for the scene of the fight, both walking
rapidly, but the tall form of Tom Glen was far
ahead of McKee. Again they came to the bear
trap. They saw nothing there but the open door
and the dangling rawhide rope now swinging
drearily in the wind. They looked down the hole.
There was the tumbled snow, splotched with blood—
some of it, surely, from Shag. Glen and McKee
stood looking down with sober faces. Then Glen
said slowly: 'Bob, you had better go on down to
the cabin. He's afraid, terribly afraid of you'.

'I know, Tom,' said McKee, moving away. 'It
makes me sick to think what a mistake I made. If
only Shag could know.'

Tom Glen followed Shag's trail for miles, but the
dog, although bleeding steadily on the snow, had,
apparently, never stopped after he ran in terror at
the sight of Bob McKee. His pace had slowed
down, but that was all. In a wild tangle of huge
rocks and burned-over timber Tom lost the trail.
All day he hunted. Almost in despair he turned
at last toward the cabin of Bob McKee, and a little
later darkness covered him; but he moved on at
the same listless stride, and his head was down as
he went.

Morning found Tom Glen hurrying with all speed away from the snowy valley. Glen had one fixed purpose—to get back to the Tamarack region and spread the news as quickly as possible. Not that the men there were now hunting Shag to kill him, but because some irresponsible person *might* try to harm him. That Old Moll was not only living, but living with Shag, would be an eye-opener to Jess Forrester as well as the rest of them. But the great pity now was that the harm to Shag's soul had been done. They had hunted with guns to kill him. He also believed, and had perfect reason to believe, that Bob McKee would destroy him.

As for Tom Glen, when he reached the valley of the Tamarack his mind was on Shag every waking hour, and often in the night he dreamed of him. Sometimes these dreams were fine, and Shag and he were romping together, and sometimes he wakened with a feeling of utter sorrow, when he had dreamed he was again lashing Shag and telling him to go away for ever.

And now Shag, instead of having enemies, had only these honest men who would go to any length to aid him—men who looked for him with eyes almost as longing as were those of Tom Glen—but the tragic thing was that Shag could not know.

CHAPTER XIII

IN THE CAMP OF THE CREES

FOR weeks Shag and Old Moll drifted north and west, never going far from the river. Night was the signal for Old Moll to halt and rest, but this was not always so for Shag. He was always hungry, and often this drove him forth in the hours of darkness.

One night Shag went farther than usual up the river in search of game. It was a night of black darkness, with snow spitting down and a savage wind roaring through the trees. In his desperation Shag ran farther and still farther in the woods along the stream. But the hours passed and he got nothing. And still he hunted as the bitter night wore on. All at once he stopped and sniffed the air. He had come to a sharp bend in the river where the timber was taller and more dense. The delicious scent of food had struck his nose. There was another smell also, but nothing like he had ever known. He made a wide detour about the place and turned back, approaching closer to the bend and near the river's edge. The strange scent that came to him

here made him understand that men were there,
but they were not the kind of men he had known.
The truth was that Shag had come upon a winter
camp of wandering Cree Indians, who had been
here hunting, trapping, and snaring their game
since late autumn.

All that Shag knew was that they were some
kind of men and that he was afraid of them. The
wigwams were in stillness so far as signs of human
life were concerned. Shag circled nearer, and
nearer still. The sleeping quarters of the Indians
loomed only as dark shadows on the snow among
the trees, and after Shag had stood near for a time
and saw nothing but the dark, silent, cone-like
things with the snow and wind hissing about them,
he concluded that so long as it was dark he might
safely search about the place for food.

Approaching very close, he passed around first
one lodge and another until he had investigated
the whole camp.

It happened that on this night old Bob McKee
was sleeping in one of the Indian lodges. Bob
knew the friendly, wandering Crees, and in days
before, when caught far from his shack with a
storm threatening, as had been the case on this
day, he had found shelter with them.

There was not one dog in this camp of the Crees.
If there had been Indian dogs in the camp they

would certainly have scented Shag, and, rushing
out at him, would have set up such an uproar that
he would have run away and so out of the danger.
As it was, there was nothing at all to frighten him.
He walked again and again around the crude
shelters of the sleeping camp.

Starving as he was, Shag still fought against the
overwhelming desire to get inside some of the
lodges for food. Yet each moment he grew more
and more desperate. He plunged through the snow
and around on the south side of a lodge. Sniffing
here, he was suddenly aware that he scented a man
whom he feared, Bob McKee. It was strange that
this man was here on this bitter night, yet it was so.

As Shag plunged through the snow about the
camp, sniffing with his nose now to this lodge and
now to that, he was more desperate than he had
yet been. As the hunger pangs gnawed he felt less
and less fear, and therefore he was less cautious.

Shag kept up his dangerous investigation at the
tepees of the Crees, mainly on the south side,
although there was little choice. A wild, roaring
wind drove so hard against the lodges, and the
snow was whirled up in such vast sheets, that it
was at times blinding. Again Shag started out in
a circle, and stopped as if he had been struck. He
scented food, and it seemed to be only a little way
out in the woods to the north. He must not lose

this precious scent. It was away from the circle of the camp, and so would be safe for him.

In a little time he was very close to the scent. He stopped for an instant close to the edge of the thicket where it was. The cunning arrangement here was nothing like anything that had ever come into his experience. But even if it had, starvation would have driven away all caution.

The truth was that Bob McKee himself had seen the young Indian, whom he knew well, trying to set this snare. It was hoped a wolf might be caught, but Bob told the young Cree he doubted it. In fact, Bob told him that nothing would come of it, that the snare was too big. But the young Cree had persisted. With the aid of Bob the two had bent down a large sapling, and by a clever arrangement of a rawhide lariat rope they had set a snare at the edge of the thicket. The Cree declared again that a wolf might be caught in this way, and he had fixed the slip-noose cunningly, just inside the thicket, in such a way that the wolf would have to put his head through the noose before he could seize the piece of meat and so spring the snare.

If Bob McKee, who now lay peacefully sleeping, had had the slightest notion of the truth here in this wild, bitter night, he would have leaped to his feet, rushed out, and at least have sprung the snare before it brought tragedy to Shag.

It was nearly morning, and it would soon be time for the sleepers to awaken. But it was still black darkness outside. The whole floor of the forest was covered with snow, but the smell of the meat told Shag where it was. The awful hunger pangs drove everything from his brain except a wild, insane desire to possess the food. He paused only for a fleeting second at the edge of the thicket, then dived in as he would have done upon game. He struck the meat with both his forepaws and his jaws. One jerk at the meat and Shag, amazed and in terror, shot up in the air as the big sapling was released. The rawhide rope bit him around the body, just behind his forelegs. In Shag's case his diving in for the meat with both jaws and forefeet saved him temporarily, for he was caught around the body, behind his forelegs, and not around the neck.

Shag did not give way to terror-stricken outcries as many dogs would have done. He was, at the moment, terror-stricken, but he throated only low, desperate sounds as he tried to struggle. At first he only pawed the air with his front feet and as futilely whipped his hind feet in the wind.

In that flash of time when Shag had felt the rope touch him he had acted instinctively, throwing himself violently back and to one side. Because of this movement, almost instantaneous with the upward swing of the sapling, Shag dangled with

THE RAWHIDE ROPE BIT HIM AROUND THE BODY

the rope at the side of his head, instead of the thing holding him directly and hopelessly from the back.

After the first shock Shag jerked his head violently to one side and tried to seize in his teeth the thing that held him, but his fangs only clashed against each other and he swayed helplessly in the biting wind. In his desperate situation there was something that kept saying to him: 'The man that once fired at you is sleeping. Don't awaken him!' Mingled with this thought was the fear that the strange men were also enemies. If they found him helpless here! This thought spurred him to frantic efforts to free himself. Then came the dawn, and he was still more frightened. Shag tried to turn his head sufficiently to get the rope in his jaws, and again and again he tried. He pawed the air in his violent efforts to turn his head enough to get the rope in his teeth, and for the first time cried out.

Again Shag struggled to get the rope in his teeth, and this time he succeeded. Then he saw one of the strange men running toward him. The young Cree who had set the snare had heard the cry that Shag had uttered. Thinking he had caught a wolf, he leaped from his blankets and came running forth. It was now daylight. It was not far to the snare, and the young Cree was almost there, when to his astonishment he heard what he knew to be the cry of a dog and not a wolf. The Indian youth was a friend to dogs. He was amazed that he had caught one in the snare, and in a flash something came to the Indian. Bob McKee had told the Crees of the great dog, Shag, that because he had proved too big and awkward, and especially because it seemed he would not fight wolves, was given away by Tom Glen, and finally hunted and harassed over hills and valleys.

'Maybe this is Shag!' the young Indian thought as he ran.

The dog was now crying—crying in mortal fear. The youth saw him. Yes! It must be the fine dog Bob McKee had told about—it must be—the great white head—and he might die in this! Acting on the instant, the young Cree climbed as quickly as he could up the sapling until it swayed and then broke beneath his weight and Shag's. Shag struck the snow in a heap, leaped up and started to run. The end of the sapling to which the rope was tied impeded him so much that the Indian ran and seized the dragging top of the sapling. He felt the jerk in his hands; at this the rope around the big, sloping chest of Shag was jerked backward as he plunged. The rope slipped back, and Shag jerked his hind legs through the noose and ran on. He had scarcely been halted when the young Cree seized the moving end of the sapling. The young Indian uttered a yell of bitter disappointment.

Almost instantly Bob McKee was out, gun in hand. To his amazement he saw the great form of Shag making away over the snow of the frozen stream.

The Indians came pouring out, and the youth told them what had happened. Bob McKee picked up the noose of the snare. There was blood on it where the rope had bitten into Shag's flesh. Then Bob stood looking down the frozen ice- and snow-covered river. Shag moved swiftly around the bend, and there was no sign of life on the frozen stream save the trail in the snow of a starving dog.

CHAPTER XIV

RATTLESNAKE COUNTRY

WINTER passed and springtime came to the land of the West. One morning Shag appeared on the summit of a hill overlooking a valley just below. There he sat down, looking pensively into the south-east. His suffering through the savage winter had in no sense taken away any of his love or his longing for Tom Glen. In fact, on this morning there had come an unusual urge to try to steal back to his old home. The peril he had been through, when many men with guns had hunted him, spoke constant warning to him, but it seemed to be getting harder and harder for him to resist this desire to steal back. To Shag, sitting high on Thunder Peak this morning, the soft breeze of spring, the green grasses of the valleys, and the flashing streams meant nothing. He could think of nothing save a man. It is more than probable that had Tom Glen appeared alone in the valley below at this moment Shag, after waiting a little to make sure Glen was alone, would have come slowly toward him. But nothing of this kind happened, and Shag kept his own counsel, the consciousness always in his brain that at any time he might see men whom he had every reason to believe were out to destroy him.

On this spring morning the sun shone soft and warm on the green valley below, and the Little Aspen River gleamed and rippled in the morning light. As Shag sat on the peak there sounded below, in the valley, the shrill neigh of a horse, and he turned his head to look. Old Moll, now with a new-born colt, stood in the valley looking up at Shag. He had left her and her colt an hour before. Shag left the high point and trotted down to the valley. Old Moll whinnied to him as he came up, and the colt walked over uncertainly toward Shag. Shag stood quietly while the colt came almost up, reached his nose out inquiringly, then stood, looking a little afraid and uncertain about the whole matter. This had happened every day, sometimes several times a day, during the life of this week-old colt.

Shag and Moll had never been away from each other any great length of time since the beginning of their strange companionship months before. When the colt came Shag did not know what to make of it, but seeing that it held so much of the interest and attention of Old Moll, he showed the same feeling of friendliness for the colt that he did for the mare. The colt, however, held some of the

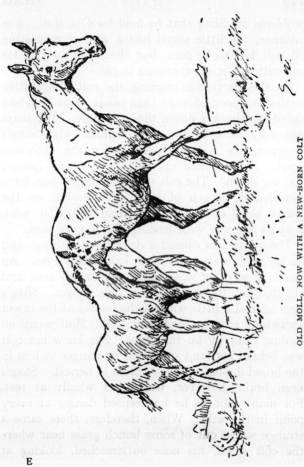

OLD MOLL, NOW WITH A NEW-BORN COLT

E

problems for Shag that he held for Old Moll. For instance, the little sorrel had a way of wandering off, not far, to be sure, but altogether too far for one with his brief experience in life.

On this particular morning the colt's inquisitive restlessness seemed more than usual. Old Moll had called him back a dozen times or more. The mare was very hungry, and now, content with Shag's presence, she fell ravenously upon the luxuriant grass. Shag walked up on a little rise of ground and lay down. The colt stood looking at him for a considerable length of time, then moved up the grassy slope of a hill-side behind Old Moll, who, busy as she was with feeding, did not see him.

The warm sun caused a drowsiness in Shag, and he lay with a sleepy, listless look in his eyes. An insect droned its way almost under his nose and alighted on the petals of a blue flower. Shag's eyes opened a little wider as he looked at the insect sprawling across the bloom. Old Moll went on feeding hungrily on the grass. She knew her colt was behind her, and suspected no danger to him in the broad daylight while so close to herself. Shag's keen brain, however, was never wholly at rest. For many months he had sensed danger at every point in the wild. When, therefore, there came a strange sound out of some bunch grass near where the colt stood, his nose outstretched, looking at something, Shag sprang to his feet. As he did so he saw the head of a snake upraised from the grass. The sound he had heard was that made by a big timber-rattlesnake that had crawled from some trees below. When Shag jumped to his feet Old Moll was startled. Swiftly Shag was at the scene.

The colt, startled by the rushing in of Shag, leaped back, and just in time, for the coiled rattler struck at him, missing his nose by a narrow margin. At this instant Old Moll, with a frightened snort, came running toward her colt. Shag had learned of these dangerous things and how to cope with them.

It was one of the most deadly of all snakes—an immense diamond rattler. Shag had killed rattle-snakes and he had developed a scheme for the dangerous work. This rattler was the largest he had ever seen, and Shag went at his work with extreme caution. The snake had no sooner struck for the colt than it whipped back into a coiled position. There, a thing of death, it raised its deadly head from the centre of its coils and waited to make Shag its victim. Old Moll, quivering by her colt, snorted and stamped in fear.

Slowly Shag circled the thing. He looked at the rattler. Its head was big, it had a knotted appear-ance about the eyes, and to Shag, from the moment the thing coiled, raised its head and shook the end of its tail with the dull, rattling sound, it all meant deadly danger. He must be quick when the rattler again struck.

Around and around the snake Shag moved, always a little out of range, then again and again he would stop suddenly and make as if he were going to drive in on the thing. These sudden moves of Shag put the rattler into a veritable frenzy of rage and fear. Twice it almost struck, but still with deadly calculation it waited for a surer opportunity.

The slope made it worse for Shag and he knew it. Each time he circled below the snake he was careful to go farther than when he circled on the upper side. When the rattler seemed fairly beside itself from the dog's sudden stops and moves, Shag began a manœuvre he afterwards became famous for. He began *running* around the snake. Around and around he ran, not close, but close enough to keep the coiled thing in a constant turmoil. Then Shag stopped abruptly and moved as if to go in; again he jerked his body as if surely this time he would drive in, and then the last straw! He did what he seldom did, barked savagely. The rattler, aflame with excitement at this, struck. The deadly fangs missed Shag's nose by a few inches. This was what he had all the time been trying to get the snake to do. In that flash of time when the rattler struck out to its full length and before it could coil again, Shag's great jaws closed upon the snake and he literally shook it to pieces. Then, after sniffing about the place for a little, he walked back to the knoll and lay down.

Old Moll, wide-eyed and trembling, and in some way knowing her colt had been in danger, led him between the knoll where Shag lay and the stream. Here she began feeding, and Shag after a time once more half-closed his eyes in the sunlight.

Evening came. As darkness settled down over the valley a brilliant moon came up, and every tree and bush stood revealed in the night. A breeze from the west stirred across the sleeping valley, and Old Moll, standing with her colt not far from Shag, did not receive any message from the wind. She only stood still, head lowered, resting in the night; but to the keen nose of Shag the low wind brought a scent, and it was the scent of food.

The breeze that brought the delicious smell to Shag's nose came from the river some distance away, and he trotted in that direction, sniffing the air as he went. Arrived at the river's edge he sniffed again, and his nose told him to go up the stream. A little farther on he stopped and turned down the sloping bank. Before him lay the waters of the river, at this point coursing around small sand-bars which lay plainly revealed in the moonlight. Along its barren slopes the evening primrose blooms had opened for the night, sending forth their delicate fragrance, which also reached the sensitive nose of Shag.

A fresh breeze brought the delicious food-smell the stronger, and pointing his nose a little up the stream, Shag splashed across the shallow water near the bank, then plunged in the deeper part and swam out to a long sand-bar. Here a half-dozen fish lay stranded and dead in what had been a small pool in the bar.

Shag was very hungry, so much so that he began at once to eat the fish. He had no suspicion there might be trouble here.

CHAPTER XV

THE GOOD COMPANIONS

SHAG was finishing the last of the fish, and his large appetite was satisfied. There was nothing about the meal that troubled him until he had nearly finished it, when as he swallowed he felt a sharp pain like something cutting in the side of his mouth, and the pain ran to his jaws. He paused momentarily, licked his lips in some trouble at this, but started to eat the remnant of the fish. When he tried to swallow there came a pain on one side of his mouth, so he left what remained and went back to the valley near Old Moll and her colt. Moll whinnied lowly to him, then again dropped her head and began dozing, while Shag, unusually restless, wandered about over the valley.

After some time he came back and lay down on the little knoll he had left when he had started toward the river and the delicious scent. But he did not long remain on the knoll, for the pain in the side of his mouth troubled him constantly. At last he coughed and tried to get rid of the foreign thing, but could not. It was a long, needle-like fish-bone that had gone into the flesh near his jaw, and Shag, like other dogs before him, was in a situation that might, in time, destroy him.

Morning came. All that day he was annoyed by the pain in his jaw. He tried to go on as usual, but the thing grew worse; at the end of a few days his jaw was badly swollen and fever was on him. He lay in a quiet little grove near the river, very sick.

It was no longer possible for him to eat even though he had felt hunger, but several times each day he managed to get down to the river and drink. Old Moll found him lying in the grove, and for a long time she stood and watched him, her colt beside her. The old mare knew that something was wrong with Shag, but she could not understand. Once she went up very close to him and put her head down until her nose almost touched him, but Shag was so sick he did not raise his head. Old Moll moved back and again began feeding in the valley, but she came back that day from time to time, and looked with dumb wonder on the great form of Shag, as he lay like one dead in the quiet grove.

At times Shag tried to fight against the sickness. In spite of his miserable condition he was still aware of his danger in the wild. Even in the springtime, when there was game to eat, there was always danger from passing grey wolves. These savage beasts were his most deadly enemies, and more than once in these nights, when he scented a wolf, he started to his feet staggering, but ready to fight as best he could. And what made this worse for him was the memory of the battle with the lobo. Shag always had a lurking fear that another beast like that might come along.

The terrible days dragged on, and at last Shag became so sick he lay one whole night unable to arouse himself. When morning came the scent of a wolf warned him, and he staggered to his feet, determined to fight if he must.

It happened that the scent of grey wolves had come to the nose of Shag for the reason that two of these beasts had chosen a den at the base of a high, rocky cliff in the mountains, not far to the north. Neither of these beasts had yet scented Shag. They both had hunted farther north and west, and the wind had been blowing almost constantly from that direction.

After sitting down for a time, Shag left the grove for water. He reached the river, lay down by the water's edge and somehow drank, but when he attempted to go back he was so weak he could not get up.

Night fell. The hours of darkness passed, and the midnight moon arose over the river. Old Moll,

* E

with her colt, came down to drink, as was her custom. She paused for a moment on the bank above until she was sure that what she saw lying near the water was Shag, and then came down the narrow cut in the bank, her colt following. As she had done so many times, she put her nose close to Shag and looked at him. For a long time after she had quenched her thirst Old Moll stood by with her colt on the sandy spot where Shag lay. And as the hours went by the mare dropped her head to look at him, still keeping her dumb vigil.

It was nearly morning when Nature touched Shag with her healing hand; the fish-bone left him, and with it the poison began to leave also. Three days passed, and he began walking about in the valley in search of food. Almost anything he could find would do, for he had lost much weight. Another week went by; Shag captured a number of rodents, and he began to put on flesh. A week after he began eating he went down the cut in the river bank and drank long and ravenously of the cold mountain water. It was more than drink now, for it put healing in his body.

The moon was up and shining brightly. The wind had veered around to the south-east, and was blowing steadily from that direction. Once Shag started with a jerk of his whole body when a small branch was blown from a tall pine and struck the moonlit

OLD MOLL STOOD BY WITH HER COLT

water. Again he went on drinking, but he was
again violently startled.   This time he whirled about
and faced the bank.   His senses were again quick
and alert for any approaching danger, but it was
only Old Moll, with her colt, coming down to the
river.

Shag stood by until she had finished drinking,
and then he and she both stood looking out into
the dark shadows across the narrow river. The
wind arose at times with a roaring through the trees
on the other side, then it died down until only a
steady, lulling sound could be heard.

Shag was not yet fully recovered from his illness,
and after a time he turned with the intention of
going into the valley to hunt. When he moved
Old Moll opened her sleepy eyes and looked at him,
and so did the colt. Shag took a few noiseless
steps toward the cut in the bank, and there came
the gentle thumping of Old Moll's hoofs behind as
she turned to follow him. Shag was now more to
Old Moll than ever, for the old outlaw-mare sensed
danger to her colt, and she also sensed in Shag
something of a protection for her offspring.

Shag had not taken more than a dozen steps
toward the cut in the high bank when there came
the sound Old Moll most dreaded, and the one that
from the first had given Shag his greatest anxiety—
the howls of timber wolves. There were two of

them, the two that hunted farther north. They had scented game, and that very much to their liking, both the mare and the colt; but in particular they desired the tender flesh of the colt.

So near were the wild howls that Shag stopped as if by an electric shock. There was no time to do anything. The wolves rushed down the bank. A great yellow and white spotted dog faced them. Thin he was, his eyes still showing his illness. Seeing this foe in their way, the two wolves rushed him at once, but as they drove in one of them swerved aside and leaped for the colt. With a frightened scream Old Moll struck at him with a front hoof, at the same time getting her colt behind her near the water.

In his full strength and power Shag could have destroyed both these timber wolves, which were only of average size, but now he was hard pressed. He fought off the first wolf and flew at the other. This beast savagely slashed at him, but Shag rushed in so hard, slashing as he went, that he drove both this brute and the other back toward the cut. Close together they faced him, and they gave ground slowly as Shag, snarling, slowly advanced. The two grey wolves turned suddenly and trotted up the bank, then, halting close to the edge of the bank above, they boldly lay down. There they remained, panting from their exertions and now and then pausing to lick their wounds. The brutes sensed that together they might destroy Shag. It was true he had wounded them, but they had also wounded him. Shag was not himself. None knew this better than he did, and it was this knowledge of his weakened condition that troubled him.

Shag dropped down on the sand and fell to panting hard. The exertion, brief as it had been, had weakened him. He was cut in a number of places, and these cuts only told him what might happen if he were forced again and again to fight. He lay watching his two enemies like a hawk. Bold as they were, the two wolves held back, and Shag still lay, miserable and anxious, as the hours of the darkness dragged by. Old Moll, standing near, now and then kicked the sand with a hind hoof, at the same time uttering a snort of fear and anger at the brazen wolves who lay above watching her and her colt.

At last daylight came. With this the two wolves left the stream, but they did not go far. When Shag went up the bank he scented them, and moving cautiously in that direction, he got near enough to see them.

Somewhat up the stream, where it wound around the base of a high cliff, Shag stood in the cover of some trees and saw both the wolves standing above on a shelf of rock. Old Moll, with her colt very close to her, was grazing in the open down the valley. Both wolves, with heads hung low, looked with sinister eyes, their tongues now and then licking their fangs. Shag moved back into the shadows of the wood, and, still anxious, made his way back down to a point near Old Moll. Presently the wind carried the wolfish scent to the mare. She was terrified by it, and started trotting away on the open land, her colt sprawling awkwardly behind her. Shag at once followed, keeping well behind the colt and stopping now and then to look back. Presently they climbed a green foothill and passed down on the other side. Here, in a narrow valley, Shag stopped, and so did Old Moll. Probably Shag knew there was no use in running far away from the two timber wolves. There were other wolves, probably, ahead. There was danger everywhere in the wild; they might as well stop here.

They had halted near a steep, narrow canyon. There was at least much grass here, and after a time Old Moll began feeding. Shag also began to hunt about for food. He hunted about until evening, getting a weasel and a rabbit, and so was satisfied. Not once during the day had he forgotten the two wolves. And something told him they would follow. They were not the kind to give up so easily. In fact, while Shag could not reason after the manner of man, he nevertheless sensed that these beasts would again try, not once, but many times, and especially under cover of darkness, to attack Old Moll and the colt. When, therefore, the night began to settle down Shag became very watchful and uneasy, pointing his nose out often to sniff the wind.

CHAPTER XVI

OLD MOLL SURRENDERS

THE sun was an hour high when Jess Forrester, after riding at an easy canter for miles, allowed his horse to slow down and pick his way along a trail near the foothills. As Jess Forrester rode on his hands dropped idly on the saddle-horn, the ever-present whip dangling from his wrist. Two things annoyed him. He had forgotten his revolver, and no one had seen Old Moll since Bob McKee had looked upon her that day running away with Shag. This had been long before. And the strange thing about it was that Shag had been seen but once since that time. Jess remembered the time, for it was he himself who had seen the dog. Shag had appeared only for a moment standing high and clear-cut on a giant boulder. But Jess had no more than seen him when he leaped down into the dense cover of a heavy pine-wood. Jess, like all the other men, knowing the truth, had called loudly to Shag, but of course it was no use.

All search about that place for Old Moll had proved futile. But spring was now come, and it was known that this unsociable old mare did sometimes graze not far from the range horses in early spring.

. As Jess rode along his mind was wholly on the mare with racing blood in her veins. He had said more than once that if he could get a good colt from her, then the wolves might take her if she insisted on running wild. And each spring for two years he had looked eagerly for a colt beside Old Moll, but in this, as in all other matters, the mare had always disappointed him.

Suddenly Jess checked his horse, and turning him aside, rode up to the remains of a horse carcass. The wolves had eaten most of it, but the keen eyes of Jess found, after a little, that this had been a black horse. It was not Old Moll. He turned and rode on, this time heading toward the Canyon River.

The early spring sun was well up in the heavens and a brooding stillness lay on the wild, rough country. Now and then a frightened bird flew up from the ground and flitted behind a tree or rock, and the blue haze of the mountains seemed farther down toward the valleys than usual. Peace pervaded all things.

As Jess rode along he presently rounded a hill and saw on the sandy margin of a *coulée* the hoof-prints of a horse and a little colt. He was intensely interested. He instantly guessed that at last Old Moll had a colt, but he knew also that wolves or mountain lions might soon destroy it, perhaps had destroyed it already.

A little farther on Jess stopped his mount abruptly and looked down on a stretch of wet sand. He saw wolf tracks mingled with those of the older horse and the colt. There was some twenty yards of this wet sand, and Jess had no difficulty in discovering that two grey wolves were following a mare and her colt, whether Old Moll or not he did not know. At the same time he thought of Shag. Where was he? Jess knew now, as did all the men of this region, that Shag had formed a kind of companionship with Old Moll in the trapping region of Bob McKee. Had the dog left Old Moll shortly after that? Or did he hunt in the vicinity she chose for herself? After the colt came had the companionship ceased? Or did Old Moll have a colt? These thoughts went through Jess's mind as he galloped along an arroyo, his eyes scanning all the country ahead of him.

All at once Jess pulled up the horse, dismounted, bent down and examined the tracks. He straightened up with a puzzled expression. 'Huh!' he exclaimed, 'either the track of Shag or another mighty big wolf! And these last tracks are very fresh. Looks as if this one was following all the others.'

Jess knew there was no certain way of distinguishing positively between the wolf and the dog tracks, when both were much the same size, yet he believed these big tracks were Shag's.

Jess mounted and cantered his horse along the draw for almost two miles. All the footprints held steady to the margin of the draw, and this continued for fully three miles, when the tracks all turned up a rocky slope. Here, after a time, Jess lost them completely. He was sitting his mount, looking toward the rock- and pine-covered knolls north of him, when his quick ears caught the sounds of what he instantly knew to be a ferocious fight. He had heard the wild, coarse snarls of a big dog and the screams of a horse. Jess put his mount at a run toward the sounds. He struck a long lane of open ground between two wooded ridges. Now he pulled his horse to a violent stop, for he knew where the fight was. The horse stood puffing as Jess leaped off and plunged up a very steep slope to a point where he could see. On the other side of a narrow, rocky canyon Jess Forrester looked, and his eyes went wide in amazement at the dramatic scene beyond.

Old Moll was backed into a small pocket of the rock ridge parallel to the gorge, trying to protect her colt beside her. There was a long, ugly slash down one side of her shoulders, and she stood quivering, her eyes bulging, at the scene before her.

The gorge was one of those narrow, sheer drops in the mountain regions scarcely fifty feet across. Jess came up behind a stunted pine and could not be seen from the other side. Never had he witnessed such a fight. It must have been in progress for some time. Shag was fighting, not one, but two timber wolves. He was slashed and bleeding, and he had been fighting three, for one wolf lay dead on the ground.

As Jess looked he saw both wolves rush Shag at once, but with lightning-like slashes Shag beat them off and backed closer to Old Moll and her little one. Then before the wolves could drive at him again he was on one of them so swiftly that he bowled him over, and at that he drove for the other. The beast whirled and ran, and the other wolf, gaining his feet, rushed behind a low thicket and beat a retreat.

His enemies gone, Shag limped up, sniffed the dead wolf, and then, crying softly, he lay down. Old Moll reached her nose down to him and uttered a low whinny. The colt stood by her side, still frightened.

It was all so intensely gripping, so swift, that Jess Forrester had for the moment been held spellbound. He had not thought, or he might have shouted and driven the wolves away. In this way he might have saved Shag some severe wounds. Jess came to himself.

'Shag! Come, Shag!' he shouted across the canyon, but at the first sound Shag started to his feet, saw the man standing beyond, and with a low cry of terror turned and loped away—away and out of sight in the rocks and pines toward the west.

'Oh, Shag!' Jess wailed, and the man's heart sank within him. He bitterly condemned himself and all the others, but it was too late. Jess plunged down the slope, mounted and turned his horse for the trail that would bring him to Old Moll and her colt.

'Shag 's afraid to come to me or any of us, and what a pity—he 's also afraid of Tom Glen. How could he be otherwise! And we believed Shag was afraid to fight wolves! Thunder and lightnin'!' And there was something fierce in Jess's voice when he said: 'Risked his life to save Old Moll and her colt—sure he did. He saw the wolves tackle the mare to kill her and the colt. And that was enough for Shag! As for the rest of us, we 're not fit to hand Shag his food. I wonder what Tom Glen will think now? But poor Tom—he 'll only feel it all the more, for no man can say too much for Shag to Tom Glen. I know what Tom 'll say when I tell him. He 'll say: "Well, Jess, knowing Shag to be the gentleman he is, could we think of him doing anything less than he did for the old mare and her colt?"'

SHAG . . . TURNED AND LOPED AWAY

'Come out of there, Old Moll.' This as Jess
came up on the other side and near the mare herself.
She still stood in the pocket with her colt. Jess
drove her and her colt forward. She seemed, for
the first time in her life, to be tractable. Perhaps
now she knew she had reason to be, under the
protection of a man. 'Get on, there!' Jess urged
her, 'and you, too, you little feller,' he said to the
colt prancing at Old Moll's side. 'You don't know
how a gentleman's just got through saving your
lives, both of you.' And then Jess went on: 'He's
never deserted *us* no matter if we did bring trouble
on him—but *we* deserted *him*.

'Get on, there, you old skinflint!' Jess shouted at
the mare, and then ceased his audible monologue
and looked seriously at the valley through which
Old Moll was now dutifully passing toward the
ranch. But as Jess's eyes looked down on the
green valley he did not see the grasses at all. He
could see nothing and think of nothing but Shag,
and he said to himself: 'As soon as I pen up the
old mare I'll get on a fresh horse and ride to Tom
Glen's. If he goes up there all alone in the morning,
maybe Shag will trust him'.

CHAPTER XVII

THE LONE WANDERER

WHILE Jess Forrester was driving Old Moll and her colt home that day Shag was alone. After covering the slopes near the Canyon River he made his way up the mountain until he came to a high, barren point. Here he stopped and looked down. In the distance his imperfect vision saw only a blur of three moving things, but he knew he saw the retreating forms of Old Moll and her colt and the man riding behind them.

Shag was so troubled that, for the moment, he could not remain still. Back and forth on the high knoll he paced, stopping often to look at the retreating form of Old Moll, going farther and farther away, and when at last he could see nothing but the distant, lonely landscape he dropped to the ground and lay very still.

Shag remained here, scarcely moving from the place, looking into the dim distance—the distance toward the south, in the somewhere of which was the home of Tom Glen. What to do now, where to go, Shag did not know. The throb and drone of life was filling all the valleys and hills. He could get his food henceforth, but the ache in his heart was always there. He was now scarred from many fights with the wolves and had just fought with them again. But his fear of them was different. He had only to be on guard, and he could take care of himself.

Toward evening Shag left the hill-top and moved away. Far up in the hills beyond the Canyon River he now hunted for food. He found all he wanted, and when his wounds healed he had no pains of the body at all, but at intervals his loneliness for Tom Glen almost overcame him. At such times he would make long journeys through forests and along the open valleys until he was again in the region of Tom Glen, but always when he neared this place Shag would come in under cover of the night. So, hunting and hiding by night and watching by day—always watching from some high, rocky cliff—he would sometimes see a rider of the range galloping along on the lower ground. On one of these occasions Shag stood quickly to his feet and cried eagerly. A horseman below galloped past and out of sight in the rough country beyond. Shag knew the rider was Tom Glen. Keeping in the cover of rocks and scrub timber, Shag hurried down to the trail, sniffed it and ran on it for some distance, and he was afraid as he ran. Then another rider appeared on a distant ridge, and Shag saw this man and Tom Glen ride away together.

Looking furtively out on the open ground, he ran behind the cover of trees and boulders, and once more got back to a high point where he could look down on the valley. Here he lay until darkness came; then making his way down to the more open ground, he trotted steadily into the north.

It was known that Shag ranged the country to the north, for every now and then some cowboy saw his great footprint in the sand along some arroyo, or in the mud beside some water-hole where Shag stopped to drink. When the big track was seen it was very properly attributed to Shag, for it was known that since the yellow lobo had been destroyed there was no other wolf of this giant size in the region. Once or twice, however, Ben Bowers, riding along and seeing the big tracks, expressed doubt, saying: 'There might be another big lobo in the region'. But when, one late afternoon, Ben saw Shag himself running like the wind across a valley for the cover of some woods, he no longer doubted.

'It 's Shag!' Ben reported to the men that night. 'It 's Shag living in the wild and still roaming along the Big Aspen.'

Tom Glen, shortly after, came up to hunt for his dog. But Shag had vanished completely. A week later the big tracks were seen miles to the north-west, not far from the Canyon River. Shag had become frightened. He was leaving the region of men.

'He 's hiding by day and doing all his hunting by night,' said Tom Glen. 'I 'm afraid he 'll never come in.'

Tom Glen went about his usual work of the range, but always the other riders noticed that his mind seemed to be preoccupied, and many times the men would see his horse tied at the foot of a mountain and Tom, high up on some barren peak, looking with his field-glasses. Sometimes they saw him riding toward home in the late evening, his hands on the saddle-horn, his horse walking, and the men knew of what Tom was thinking. Although silent Tom Glen did not speak of it, the men knew that his mind must be on Shag, and in particular that night when Shag had gone into the death fight with the lobo.

These summer days slipped by, and now for more than three weeks not even a footprint nor a sign of Shag had been seen by the men. He seemed to have left the country utterly.

Late August came. Yellow and purple cone-flowers bloomed in the hush of sequestered valleys, and beautiful starry asters held silent vigil in a land breathing farewell to summer.

The days passed into early October, and a solemn hush lay on hill and plain. And still as the riders passed through the hills and valleys not one sign of Shag was to be seen.

'He's gone out of the country,' they said. 'We'll never see him again.' But Tom Glen would not give up. He still rode, watchfully, hopefully, looking for the big track near his horse or gazing everywhere in the distance that the familiar form might be seen.

CHAPTER XVIII

IN SIGHT OF HOME

In these days of autumn the crows were cawing in the trees of the ravines and the woods along the streams. The redbird's clear whistle broke the stillness of the distant woods, over which a blue haze hung like a misty veil.

One morning, as the sun rose, Shag came trotting over a ridge and swung into a little wood. Once again he was back to the Tom Glen region. Shag was tired. Screened by some thickets, he lay flat on his back and allowed the sunshine that filtered through the trees to fall upon him. But in a very short time clouds covered the sun, and all the sky and the air was so chill that Shag got up.

Already on this morning he had been uneasy, for three times he had seen horsemen in the distance. Shag had come here a number of times, and had grown used to their ways. By clever turns and quick running he had learned to keep out of sight while watching for Tom Glen. It was not that Shag would run out to meet Tom Glen if he saw him. The fear of other men, who had once hunted him, would have prevented this. But he longed to see the man he loved.

Shag kept well under cover all that day, and nothing happened. When night came he got what food he needed, but when he lay down to rest this chill November night he was uneasy. He was sure he was now seeing more men riding the range than usual. But he would not leave the place.

Once Shag saw what the men were looking for, several grey wolves. The beasts were running in a pack on a plain below a hill where Shag stood, but he had seen so many wolves that this meant nothing unusual to him.

CHAPTER XIX

THE RING HUNT

ALTHOUGH it was late autumn, there had as yet been but little snow. Horses and cattle, however, were brought in nearer the ranches.

Some time before a pack of wolves had come down from the north and had begun to harass both horses and cattle. Finally, one night these wolves killed five steers and three young horses. This put the fire of battle in the range men. At least six grey wolves had been seen in one pack, and there might be more. They would be so dangerous to the cattle and horses that something must be done at once, while hunting could be done on horses.

It was the keen mind of Tom Glen that offered the plan of a great ring hunt to bring down the wolves. Being already late autumn, winter might set in at any time with a savage storm. Therefore the hunt should be organized quickly. Tom Glen laid his plans and the news spread like wildfire. Not only the younger men, but the old ones as well,

looked to the perfect working of their rifles, and on
the fourth day after the word had gone out from
Tom Glen scores of riding men were dotting hills
and valleys at widely separated points, all having a
common objective—to move watchfully toward the
great lone pine in the valley of the Tamarack.
With the men were dogs to the number of nearly
two score. These followed their masters, trotting
along in twos and threes at widely separated points
in the great 'ring'.

'If every man watches and is ready,' Glen told
them, 'we should get some of these wolves before
they break through the circle.'

The day before this hunt, having seen no more
men in the vicinity to the south, where he so much
longed to be, Shag trotted out of the woods, and
by midnight he was well down in the Tom Glen
region. He fed well that night, and a little later
the late moon found him on a high hill, looking
toward the south and sniffing the breezes. The
danger seemed to have passed again, and as morning
approached he took shelter in a belt of creek woods,
where he curled up and went to sleep.

During these hours there was hardly a sound
to break the stillness. Shag slept peacefully on.
Slowly the daylight came, and it came with a
cloudy sky and a threat of storm.

The time slipped by. Shag opened his eyes and

F

HE CURLED UP AND WENT TO SLEEP

looked up. An owl, flying silently, alighted on a limb overhead. It was daylight. For a moment Shag looked at the owl lazily, then he suddenly sprang to his feet in fear, his eyes gleaming, his whole body tense with excitement. He had heard disturbing noises to the north of him—the hum of human voices and the beat of horses' hoofs as they struck the hard ground. To Shag these were unmistakable danger signals.

Swiftly he ran through the intervening woods and peered cautiously through the fringe of trees at three horsemen and a number of long-legged hounds. After these had passed Shag wanted a better cover. He ran down along the creek side where the woods were thicker. A half-mile of running, and again he stopped to listen. He heard no sound, and being thirsty, stopped to rest and to lap a little of the creek water.

Again he stole down through the woods, and again was brought to a sudden stop by the sound of men's voices close at hand. Again Shag decided to lie low, on the chance that they would pass him. His ruse was successful. Safely under cover, he watched them until they had ridden beyond him to the foot of a hill. They were now moving away from his hiding-place, and he was just beginning to feel a bit easy, when again he was greatly startled by loud cries close at hand, and looking out, saw that his enemies—he had every reason to believe them so—were coming back!

He stood still, head up, and listened intently where some trees screened him.

The voices now were much nearer. His pursuers had turned, and were coming directly through the woods along the creek, and on the grassland bordering both sides of the stream he saw riders and hounds. There was only one thing to do—run with all speed through the woods to the north.

Shag broke into a run under the cover. Things looked black enough, and Shag made no mistake in believing the many hounds he saw would be deadly once they saw him. They would tear him to pieces if they could, but this very great danger to Shag was one not thought of by the men, and it was only Tom Glen who even hoped that on this hunt he might get a glimpse of Shag.

Shag ran until he came to a turn, where another ravine dipped into the creek. He headed up the gorge at a run, turned, ran up the ravine side, gained the trees at the edge, and waited. Things looked better, for the horsemen were all riding well on the other side of the ravine. If they kept in that direction Shag would lie quietly where he was and let them go on. By doing this, although he did not know, he would thus have slipped through the gigantic ring at the very outset and so made his escape. But it was not to be so. When a little time had passed, three horsemen with a number of hounds again rode into the ravine from below, two of them riding along in the bottom of the gorge, a third on the upper side, moving directly toward the place where Shag was hiding.

CHAPTER XX

BEFORE THE BLIZZARD

SHAG took no further chance, but looking swiftly around him, made for the sharp hill-ridge straight ahead—his only hope for freedom. In a flash he was in the open, and almost immediately he gained the ridge, passed over it, and ran down the long hill without having been seen. The men, busy with talking, and because of the overhanging branches of trees and the many boulders projecting on either side the gorge, had not caught sight of him.

Shag raced like the wind till he reached a ravine at the foot of the long slope, where again there were trees. Here he broke into a lope.

Running quickly up the north side of the ravine, and looking north-eastward, he saw on a hill-top, far in the distance, several horsemen riding hard toward the west. This was toward the place where he had so lately been, and it alarmed him anew. He at once ran down the ravine, hoping he might now slip away under cover. Never in his life had Shag seen so many men and hounds. He was

growing desperate. And now he must use all his
cunning. In a running fight, with not too many
pursuers, he could still escape, but the number was
appalling, and there was no point where he could
break through. His heart throbbed wildly and a
fierce gleam was in his eyes. He must not be
caught! Rapidly through the woods of this ravine
he ran toward the east.

Suddenly he was greatly startled by a wolf which
came running toward him under the trees, and then
shot past him. Shag halted only for an instant,
for ahead of him the thump, thump of many
horses told only too plainly that escape in his
present direction was cut off. He turned back
to follow the wolf, but the wily animal was out of
sight.

Shag ran on to the end of the ravine. He saw
two wolves running in the open to the west.

Suddenly, amid loud yelling by the men, a dozen
hounds from two different directions shot down the
valley toward the fleeing wolves. At the same
time another loud uproar arose from the west.
Shag tarried only long enough to see the wolves
surrounded by hordes of yelling men and plunging,
snapping hounds. He had no thought of waiting
to see the outcome. He was surrounded on three
sides, but there was still a slim chance for escape, a

small draw leading out from the ravine covered with tall, dead grass.

Shag heard more of the men now rushing pell-mell up through the ravine behind him. Each moment they were drawing nearer. Ahead, it seemed, certain death awaited him. From the south horsemen and other dogs were coming up. Only one way, the little draw covered with tall, dead grass, offered. This promised little, but Shag, desperate, took the chance. He did not run down the draw, but crouching low, moved along until he came to the edge of the tall grass cover. Directly in front of him were horsemen and hounds, moving swiftly and surely toward his hiding-place. Dogs of many breeds were coming, dogs that had fought him in his worst days of trouble.

Now he was surrounded on all sides, and no matter which way he turned he must run the gauntlet of these hunters. Crouching in the dead grass, his body tense, he waited. He knew he could not escape from the draw unseen. His pursuers, with tremendous odds in their favour, were now almost upon him; there was only one thing to do—crouch low in the grass and wait. Not a sound escaped him. Louder and louder rang out the noise of pounding hoofs and the shouts of the men as they came on. Shag still held his position with the enemy dotting the land about him. He moved not a muscle. His throat was dry; once he licked his fangs quickly.

Watching with fiery, bloodshot eyes, Shag waited until horsemen and hounds were very near. Directly in front came the two hounds of Tom Glen that always had set upon him, one of them the big, grizzled black dog, but they were now with Ben Bowers. In a moment these two hounds were in the widest opening between the horsemen. This gave Shag a chance; he took it. Leaping from the cover with a never-to-be-forgotten rush, he shot for the opening. In a flash one of the big deer-hounds cut in. Shag drove straight at him, throwing up his head in the old way as he struck. The men were astounded. The big hound was bowled completely over from the shock, but Shag kept his feet, slashed once at the hound, shot clear, and ran free from the wide circle, and every man recognized him! 'It's Shag!' they roared.

In the twinkling of an eye dogs and horsemen whirled, and for half a mile the plain was a howling mob of frenzied men and racing hounds. Jess Forrester's heart went sick, as did Tom Glen's and that of every man.

Shag could gain nothing by dodging, for no matter which way he turned there came an enemy

* F

ready to cut him off. These hounds could no more be stopped than wolves could be stopped.

The speed of Shag was remarkable. He outdistanced the foremost hounds, but the long, oncoming line following close behind, which compelled a straight-ahead run to the east, troubled him greatly. If cut off from the east he must turn, and whether he turned to right or to left a score of gleaming fangs awaited him.

A quarter of a mile was passed, and still the gap between Shag and his pursuers was not lessened. The swiftest of the hounds had not been able to gain a single foot. Shag and hounds topped a small knoll. Before him lay a broad stretch of table-land. Still leading the storm of death that swept after him he shot across the level grassland.

The din and confusion increased in fury—the thundering hoof-beats of the horses, the cracking of whips, the shouts of the horsemen.

Another half a mile, and still Shag kept the lead; and now, had not something unlooked for happened, he might have escaped. But all at once, about a hundred yards away, from a deep gully toward the north-east, a belated horseman and three hounds appeared. This man, too, recognized Shag, and he, after the first instant, joined the others as his own dogs became unmanageable. Shag, hard pressed

by the neighing of the horses, thus
lessening the chance of meeting an enemy
on that...

"Upset as he was, rather than ride him
behind, thirty yards with a plaintive dea-
Bonny, to the leaders drew faster, slipped
after all the mighty man...crashed
and dived.

Shag was ... and struck by the
... and struck his ... his tongue
... savagely, his
... the big
... had been
... but ... The high
... but...

... something went
... Things helped
... been felt the swift
... vexation
... he was
... and of
... the horses.

... the sound of ... other
... riders ... ... their
... horses at top speed ... up to the
... land. The ...huge
... grass... swept... across the

STILL SHAG KEPT THE LEAD

by the new hounds, swerved to the right, thus lessening the gap between himself and the enemy on that side.

Urged on by the shouts of the men, rather than halted thereby, the hounds, with a big black deerhound in the lead, put on a new burst of speed. Shag, at the moment swerving to the right, crashed into this dog.

Shag was whirled completely around by the impact, but still he kept his feet and, turning, struck like a cat. Twice he chopped savagely, his fangs slashing deep into the muscles of the big hound. In another instant he would have been free, but three other hounds closed in. The fight was furious, but brief.

His fangs chopping, while in an unending whirl he slashed his way through the circle, Shag leaped away, and again was running free. At the sight Jess Forrester let out a wild yell of admiration. As for Tom Glen, he could not speak, and there was a mist in his eyes. Now Tom Glen was ahead of all the horsemen.

The sound of the shouting men reached other belated riders in the lower levels. Spurring their horses at top speed, they tore madly up to the high land. The race now took on the proportions of a great cavalcade sweeping swiftly across the table-land after the great Shag. He was still ahead, but inwardly groaning under the strain.

Just ahead of him loomed a deep gully with a sheer drop of three feet which could not be seen by the horsemen, because of the bordering tall, dead grass, until they were actually upon it. With one leap Shag cleared the draw, and without the least slackening of speed he raced up the opposite hill. At this moment a number of near-spent horses plunged over the side of the gully and fell, hurling their riders over their heads to sprawl in the sand beyond. A long line of hounds, brindle, blue, black, yellow, floundered for an instant in the sand where they had tumbled. But the big black deer-hound and a dozen others had already cleared the gully and raced up the hill, hot on the trail of Shag.

On the hill-top they circled and again closed in on him. But the halt was not a complete one. Most of the hounds in at the start of the race had now dropped out, utterly spent. Another quarter of a mile, and at last Shag was breaking under the terrific strain. Slowly the hounds began closing the gap between them, and finally the big black deer-hound, which still kept the lead, again closed in; but Shag whirled and beat him back.

Again a running fight was on, with Shag fighting desperately on all sides save the front, which for a time he kept clear. He fought savagely until they reached a little bare knoll overlooking a steep, rocky incline which, far down in the woods, ended in the bed of a little creek. Here the few hounds that were up surrounded him and he made a last stand. Tom Glen and the men, now on jaded horses, seemed pitifully far away.

In the valley below the light was already fading under a dark and stormy sky. Overlooking the valley on the north a bald eagle, perched on a crag, turned its head and looked down upon the scene. A hawk, poised high in the air, hung silently, then swung in wide circles out over the valley. In the woods below a crow uttered one loud caw, then stopped short as if frightened at the impending calamity.

Twice Shag went down in a whirl of dust on the knoll, but he was instantly up again, rushing and slashing and whirling. His coat was covered with blood and a crimson stream trickled slowly from both his shoulders. The big black hound rushed hardest upon him. Had this dog been alone Shag would have destroyed him.

For a moment the fight was on the edge of the very steep incline. With that agility that never deserted him Shag met the attack of the black hound and drove in on him so violently that when he struck he knocked him over the steep, lost his own footing, and went over also.

Tom Glen, Jess Forrester, and old Bob McKee were now up. As Shag went over, the three men swiftly leaped down from their panting horses, ran up to the edge of the steep and looked down.

Over and over rolled Shag and the hound. The two were well apart, both as helpless as two rolling stones. Half-way down the hound crashed into a clump of bushes and lay still. But Shag rolled on and on, striking nothing until he bumped against the bushes at the edge of the wood. At once he got to his feet, moved uncertainly, and fell. Once again he got up, and this time he staggered off out of sight among the trees.

The men moved around the steep and got down to the little stream. Near the bank of the creek they came upon Shag's tracks, deep crimson stains showing where he had paused to drink.

Tom Glen leading, they followed the crimson trail a little farther. Along the muddy bank bloody footprints showed where the sufferer had been moving.

At this moment young Len Pitts came up and, swinging himself from his horse, led his mount as

the other men were doing. Young Len walked
close to Tom Glen.

After some time the trail led out of the woods,
along the stream, to a valley dotted with many
thickets and low draws in which grew scrub timber
and tall, dead grasses.

As Tom Glen and young Len Pitts looked out on
this grey landscape both gave a start, for both saw
Shag, but saw him only for a flash as he passed
out of sight into one of the draws.

All of the horsemen were now up. The north
wind came down with chilling blasts, and scattering
particles of snow and sleet began spitting across the
valley. It was late. Night would come very soon
and a storm was coming. The cutting wind with
hissing sleet drove harder against horses and men.

'Wait till morning, Tom,' Jess Forrester urged
him, but Tom Glen shook his head.

'All of you go down to my ranch for the night,'
he said. 'Len here says he must stay with me.
You know Shag's afraid of all of you. Len and I
will try till it's night, then we'll come.'

The protests made by the men because of the
coming storm were of no avail. And while they
galloped toward the ranch of Tom Glen, Tom and
young Len Pitts rode westward toward the place
where they had for a moment seen Shag. As Tom

started away he said to Len kindly: 'Len, don't you think you had better go with the men? The storm may be bad'. But Len Pitts would not leave him. 'You may need me, Tom,' he said. 'I think Shag may come to us two—and I 'm afraid he 's badly hurt.'

CHAPTER XXI

RETURN OF A HERO

THE biting wind, with a stinging sleet, put high spirit in the two horses of Tom Glen and Len Pitts. Twice they shook their heads and whirled about in protest at facing the stinging gale. Already the day was growing darker.

Tom Glen had seen Shag disappear in a dip in the ground where there was a long draw bordered with tall, withered grasses and thickets.

A little later the two riders reached the draw, and in the biting sleet they rode up and down on the level ground above the place, searching the grass and calling the name of Shag. He was not there.

At the extreme south end of the draw that ended in a blind pocket was a low, overhanging ledge of rock. Glen thought it possible Shag might be lying under the ledge. It was necessary to dismount to get down in the hollow to look. Tom Glen, with a piece of lariat rope in his hand with which he intended to tie Shag, if he found him, dismounted.

Both horses were now highly nervous. As Glen attempted to hand his bridle-reins to Len Pitts in the face of the driving storm both mounts plunged together, and Len Pitts, excellent horseman though he was, just touched the reins when his horse shot aside and from under him. Len picked himself up, and to the consternation of both riders, their horses thundered away down the plain to the south.

Tom leaped down in the hollow and looked under the ledge. Shag was not there. As Glen climbed up to the level there came a dense rushing blast of sleet and snow that cut like fire. Glen and Len Pitts started at a run toward a distant pine-wood, the only shelter for miles. The hollow behind them was impossible as a refuge, facing the north as it did. They had covered only a little distance when the snow and sleet came driving down in appalling blasts, and with this a roar that warned them both of the danger. One of those deadly things of death of the old West was upon them—a blizzard.

Suddenly, out of the dark gloom where things could scarcely be seen, both men stumbled to their knees as they ran against something, and Tom Glen shouted: 'Len! It 's Shag!' Then both Glen and Len Pitts had their hands on him, and Shag was crowding close to Tom Glen and crying. 'It 's Shag!' shouted Glen again, at the same time

RN OF A HERO

wondering whether any of them would live through
this thing. On the instant Tom tied the rope to
Shag's neck, and in doing so his hands encountered
ugly wounds and frozen blood. Glen, holding the
rope in one hand and Len by the other, started in
the wild confusion of the storm.

Why Shag came to Tom in this storm can never
be known. Some thought that Shag had seen the
men and dogs move away toward the south, and
also had seen Tom Glen and Len Pitts come on
alone toward the west. Probably this was so.
Shag knew as well as the men that the storm was
a dangerous thing. If he had thought only of his
own safety in escape he surely could have reached
the woods, badly wounded though he was. Yet
he chose to come to Tom Glen. Shag cried a little
at first, but now he was running ahead and pulling
so hard on the rope that it was plain to Glen that
he had his mind bent on some particular objective.

Tom Glen and Len Pitts had dressed for a chill
day of riding, but when the biting blasts struck
them the cold seemed to cut to the bone. They
grasped each other's hands and shouted that they
must try to keep together. All they knew was
that they were running and stumbling with the
storm, and they knew this must be southward.
There was scarcely a moment when Glen did not

feel Shag pulling at the rope, although he could not see him in the howling darkness. They were now on top of a low ridge which gradually sloped southward for a quarter of a mile to level land, but they did not know this. The ranch-house was still three miles away, and it seemed impossible that they could stumble upon it in such a raging sea of death. But perhaps Shag would lead them to some other cover, they thought.

Glen shouted in Len Pitts's ear: 'I must hold to you, Len, and you must keep with me and Shag! He's still pulling on the rope!'

Glen thought hard as they ran. There was only one way, and that was to run before the storm. No living being could face it and live. Both Glen and Len Pitts knew of men getting lost in the open during these storms who were found later frozen to death. Once Glen thought that if the worst came to the worst he and Len and Shag could lie down in the hope that the snow would drift over them and keep them from freezing, but this would be a most dangerous experiment, as they would likely be frozen before they were sufficiently covered with snow on this open plain.

All at once Glen stumbled, lurched forward and fell. His hands and arms plunged down in the snow around some obstruction, and his head grazed a stump. The fall did not render him unconscious, but he felt the pain and shock of it. As he fell he let loose the rope holding Shag. 'Shag's gone!' he thought as he fell; but while he was struggling to get up Glen heard a whine in his ear and felt Shag's tongue on his cheek. Again he got hold of the rope; fortunately Len had stopped the instant Glen had fallen. Their hands had separated, but by shouting and feeling, they were so near they got together again.

With the incessant roar almost complete darkness fell. As Glen struggled to his feet there sounded in their ears, muffled yet distinct, the coarse bark of a big dog. 'Shag's pulling again on the rope,' Glen shouted in the ear of Pitts, 'we'll let him have his way!'

It seemed as if they had been running an age, when both Glen and Len Pitts fell, but only to their knees. Instantly in the roar and the darkness Shag, feeling the rope slacken, was back and close to Tom Glen.

Again they started, Shag pulling steadily on the rope. At last Tom shouted to Len; there was despair in his voice: 'Len, I'm afraid we've passed the ranch-house. If only Shag could lead us to a gorge or—something!'

On and on they ran. 'Surely,' thought Glen,

'we have passed the only hope—the ranch-house.'
Young Len Pitts had said nothing. He had a
feeling deep in him that Shag knew what he was
doing. Then all at once Glen felt that Shag had
turned—yes, he *had* turned toward the left, and it
was terrible to fight across the blinding sleet and
snow. It was all Glen and Pitts could do to keep
on their feet now, for it had been bad enough going
down with the storm.

'We can't stand this long!' Glen shouted, 'and if
Shag 's wrong——' His words were drowned in
the storm. They followed on. Then Glen shouted
that they should pull Shag back and go with the
wind.

'No! No! Listen, Tom! Listen!' shouted young
Len Pitts. 'Shag 's going in the right direction.
Listen!'

Glen was shocked. He thought Len was in
delirium from it all.

'Hear what!' Glen shouted.

'Listen!' Len Pitts screamed close to Tom Glen.
'The shots—hear the shooting! It 's the men at
the ranch-house—trying to make us hear!'

Glen then for the first time noted the sounds.
They were strangely muffled in the awful roar—
shots coming from heavy rifles, but sounding faint
and distant in this now black night of rushing death.

And Shag, in this never-to-be-forgotten hour, was still fighting directly across the storm toward the ranch-house, and he had turned before any man or gun had guided him.

In that moment of threatening death the whole thing came to Tom Glen. Shag had guided them down an almost perfectly level stretch of valley that led somewhat west of the ranch. Here, now, after taking advantage of the best of the ground, the dog had turned half in the face of the storm, and he was leading two helpless human beings toward life—not death.

The shots seemed nearer. Glen knew they would be muffled even though one was very close to the firing.

Suddenly, in the black night of roaring storm, Shag barked quick and sharp. The next moment the door of the ranch-house opened; Tom Glen and Len Pitts stumbled inside and fell, too exhausted to rise. Shag crowded close to Tom Glen and licked his face and cried and cried. The men came close to lift up Glen and Pitts, but Glen waved them back and put his hand on Shag.

'It 's all right, Shag!' Glen told him as Shag lay now with his head low to the floor, crying and still crying, in spite of all that Glen could do or say to him. Tom got up on his knees and so did Len, and they put their hands on the dog with the ugly frozen wounds upon him. Tom Glen put his head down very close to Shag, and talked to him as a father talks to a child who has been badly hurt by those he trusted.

Len Pitts pulled his old red handkerchief from his pocket and dashed the tears from his eyes. In an unsteady voice he told the men how Shag had led him and Tom Glen in. When Len finished there was dead silence in the room of more than twenty men, silence save for the now low, moaning cries of Shag. He lay on the floor with Tom Glen's hands upon him and Tom Glen's voice trying to soothe him. And after a time Shag's cries grew lower and lower, and with Tom's voice still speaking words in his ears Shag fell asleep. Tom raised a sober face and nodded toward one of the bunks for a blanket. Ben Bowers and a dozen men started for it, but Ben was first. He handed Tom the blanket, and Tom very slowly and tenderly eased it under Shag's head. Shag roused up and started to cry, but when he saw Tom Glen still beside him he fell asleep again. The men brought Tom a blanket, and he lay down beside Shag. Finally Len Pitts lay down, and was soon asleep.

All night the storm roared on with unabated fury. At times the ranch-house shook and quivered in

the face of the driving wind. All night some of
the men sat at one end of the room near the fire-
place, and time after time they lifted wood to the
fire. When this was done, they sat silently looking
at the still form of Shag and at Tom Glen, his head
resting on his arm, fitfully sleeping beside him. At
times the wind shook the ranch-house so fiercely
that the men looked at one another uneasily; then,
when there came the steady roar again, they sat
looking at the form of a great dog lying so still on
the floor. Now and then one of the men would
steal over on tiptoe and look down upon Shag,
and then slip back again and resume his vigil with
the others.

Twice during the night Tom Glen was awakened
by the touch of Shag's paw on his face. Shag
made no sound, but it was plain to Glen that the
dog was suffering, and he seemed to be trying to
say something.

All that night Glen never left him. When
morning came Shag was very ill and his wounds
were bleeding again. Not a man would leave the
ranch, and all were constantly trying to think of
something more they could do for him. It was a
strange thing that when any of these men now
came into the room where he lay they took off
their hats. They were men unused to removing

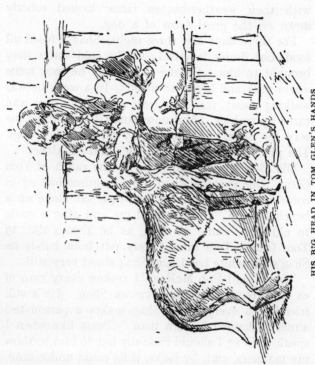

HIS BIG HEAD IN TOM GLEN'S HANDS

their hats, and not one did it because he saw another do so; but the hats came off as these uncouth men, with their weather-beaten faces, looked soberly down on the great form of a dog.

For three days and three nights Shag refused all food, but drank feverishly of the cold water they brought to him. On the fourth day he took some warm milk and began to mend. In a week he was walking about, ready to greet any of the men who came up to him. And now Tom Glen went all the way for Shag. He gave away all his other dogs. The place henceforth was Shag's and his alone.

Old Bob McKee stayed on at the ranch of Tom Glen. One evening when the springtime had again come to the valley these two men sat alone on a bench outside. Shag walked up, and after a smile to old Bob, came at once, as he always did, to Tom Glen. Tom immediately put both hands on Shag's big white head, and Shag stood very still.

'Tom,' said Bob McKee, 'I reckon every man of us is better because he's known Shag. He's still friendly to everybody. Shag makes a person feel almost ashamed he *is* a man. 'Pears like when I speak to Shag I should raise my hat to him to show my manners, and, by jacks, if he could understand, I *would* raise my hat to him!'

But Shag only stood with his eyes closed, his

big head in Tom Glen's hands, and Glen and McKee sat still on the bench. It was late. The sun had set and shadows were creeping over the plain. Tom Glen did not reply, but only held his hands a little closer on Shag's head. Neither Shag nor the men moved, and each was with his own thoughts. Deeper and deeper the shadows fell, until at last the silence of night came over the valley.